Immortal Love

Carmen Ferreiro-Esteban

Crimson Romance
New York   London   Toronto   Sydney   New Delhi

CRIMSON
ROMANCE

Crimson Romance
An Imprint of Simon & Schuster, Inc.
1230 Avenue of the Americas
New York, NY 10020

ISBN 978-1-4405-5476-6
ISBN 978-1-4405-5477-3 (ebook)

Dedication

TO GUSTAVO ADOLFO BÉCQUER AND FEDERICO GARCÍA LORCA, MY TWO
FAVORITE POETS, WHOSE LIVES, SO TRAGICALLY SHORT, I HAVE EXPANDED IN
MY NOVEL, BY GRANTING THEM IMMORTAL BODIES.

AN IMMORTALITY THAT, IN SPIRIT, THEY HAVE ALREADY ATTAINED THROUGH
THEIR WORK.

TO MARIE AND THE MEMBERS OF BILY (BECAUSE I LOVE YOU) AT DOYLESTOWN.

MY FAMILY OUTSIDE MY FAMILY. I WOULDN'T HAVE MADE IT WITHOUT YOU.

TO MY CRITIQUE GROUP, THE PAPER WHITES, WHO READ IT FIRST.

Chapter One: Bécquer

Bécquer called Sunday morning.

I was arguing with my daughter at the time, because she wanted to go to a Halloween party and I said no. I said no, not only because the party started late, but also because the outfit she planned to wear would have been too small had she been five, and she was fifteen. Caught in the middle of my impassioned speech to support my refusal, I picked up the receiver and barked a sharp hello.

A voice, deep and beguiling, answered mine. "Carla, this is Bécquer."

The dark eyes his name evoked sent my heart into overdrive so that my voice shook when I returned his greeting.

"We met last Sunday at the Eastern College Writers Conference," he explained.

As if I could forget.

He had been the only agent to ask me for a full manuscript that day. The only male, too, in a sea of female agents, a fact that would have made him memorable even if he hadn't had the impossible good looks of a pagan god. He was older than most agents at the conference, mid-thirties was my guess, and, unlike all the others, he knew who I was.

"I read *Two Moon Princess*," he'd told me when I sat down at his table. His voice, loud enough to be heard over the noise of other attendees furiously pitching their stories, was warm, creating a comforting intimacy between us. An intimacy his words only enhanced.

He was the fifth agent to whom I'd delivered my pitch that morning. Or maybe he was the sixth. I'd lost count of how many had told me already, with canned smiles glued on their faces, that my project was not a good fit for their list. As for someone reading my published work, that was a first. Ever.

"You did?" I mumbled, trying to remember whether I had sent a resume with my application.

"I ran a search on you." He answered my unspoken question. "I'm interested in Spanish history." Nothing personal, his words implied.

"Your accent—"

"Still there after all these years," he interrupted me as if to discourage further inquiry. "Tell me about your new novel. Did the boy kill the queen?"

"It's a love story," I told him, reluctant to give away the ending.

Bécquer smiled, showing a perfect row of white teeth between his sensuous lips. "Marvelous. I adore love stories, especially when they have tragic endings."

Bécquer's voice came through the phone, bringing me back to the present. "I finished your manuscript and would like to meet with you to discuss it. If that's all right."

"Yes, of course." I tried and failed to sound nonchalant. "When?" I grabbed a pen as I spoke and faced the calendar on the kitchen wall to mark the date.

"Café Vienna on State and Main in fifteen minutes?"

"Fifteen minutes? You mean you're here in Doylestown?"

"Exactly."

I would have asked for more time, but I could hear Madison screaming her head off up in her room, probably complaining to a friend about her impossible mother. Because my mind was busy blocking her voice, I didn't have a lot of brains left for thinking. So I agreed, only to panic as soon as I hung up.

What was I thinking? I would never make it on time.

But I did. It took me a minute to run upstairs, give Madison an ultimatum—either she could go to the party in another costume or wear that one at home—and rush in, then right back out of my room.

*

Bécquer was sitting by one of the windows, a cup of coffee in front of him. He got up as I approached and, after inviting me to the chair across from him with a movement of his hand, asked me what I would like to drink.

"An espresso would be nice," I said, taken aback by his old-fashioned manners. When was the last time someone, male or female, had offered to get my order? Yes, I knew gentlemanly manners were a sign of male dominance, and I had endured enough of the drawbacks of a misogynistic society as a child to be certain I didn't want to live in one. But the way Bécquer asked was not condescending, more like offering a courtesy to an equal. If he wanted to impress me, he succeeded. Somehow, I thought he wasn't trying.

Soon he was back from the counter and set the espresso in front of me: a small cup on a saucer, the European way. I thanked him for the coffee and for the fact that he had brought me a real cup. How did he know, I wondered, that I missed the Spanish cafés and the coffee served like this, in white porcelain cups? Maybe he missed them, too, and he had guessed.

How strange the little things I remembered from my old life, the one I gave up when I followed my ex-husband to the States. I shook my head to get rid of the memories, and sipped my coffee while Bécquer stared at me.

"I loved your story," he said, when I put the cup down.

I waited, out of habit, for the "unfortunately it doesn't fit my current list" I was certain would follow, but it didn't come.

"I hope you don't have an agent yet, for I would like to represent you."

"You want to represent me?"

"Yes, of course. You didn't think I came all the way here to apologize for not taking you as a client, did you?"

"No, I suppose not."

"I trust you have checked my credentials by now and know I've run my agency for ten years and been pretty successful placing my clients."

7

He laughed when I blushed, for he had guessed right.

"So?"

I knew I had a speech prepared for this occasion stored somewhere in my brain. But when I searched my mind I couldn't find it. I nodded. "Yes, I would like you to be my agent."

"Good." Bécquer reached for the briefcase resting on the windowsill. He had beautiful hands, wide and strong, an artist's hands. Long ago, when I was younger, I had looked at hands as a way to judge a possible suitor. Bécquer's would have passed the test big time. Not that it mattered anymore. I was not thinking of a suitor now. Hadn't since I'd married. Not even after the divorce. When you marry the devil you don't want to try again.

"Are you all right?"

I blushed furiously under his dark stare and nodded.

Bécquer pushed a paper toward me. "I took the liberty of bringing the contract with me. Care to sign?"

"Now?"

"After you've read it, of course."

An alarm went off in my head. Every piece of advice I had ever heard told me to be cautious, to read the small print. But when I looked down and saw the contract, I frowned in surprise. It was handwritten, with the flowery calligraphy they don't teach in schools anymore. A style that would have been outdated, even in my time. Yet it was easy to read: the text was short and straightforward, the conditions better than the ones on a standard contract. No fine print to ponder.

I looked up. "It seems reasonable," I said, and then stopped, suddenly aware of the total silence around us. Everyone, I realized with a start, was frozen in place, as if they were actors in a movie I had paused by mistake.

"What happened?"

"Beatriz." Bécquer pointed at the door where a woman in a smart suit stood facing us. "My personal secretary. She found me."

My stomach hurting as if the coffee I'd just swallowed had turned to ice, I looked from the woman back to him, and then again around us, taking in the impossible stillness of the place.

"Who are you?" I asked, my voice broken with fear.

Bécquer sighed and raised his hands in a gesture of surrender.

"I'm Bécquer," he said. "Gustavo Adolfo Bécquer."

He pronounced the name slowly, his eyes on mine, and I knew he wasn't lying. Yet the truth was unacceptable.

"You may remember me from your Spanish classes," he continued. "*Literatura* it was called back then, if I'm not mistaken."

"That's impossible."

I stood so abruptly my chair crashed to the floor. I remembered Bécquer, all right. He was the Spanish writer whose poems of unrequited love I'd memorized when I was thirteen, as every other Spanish girl, before and after me, has done the first time a clueless boy breaks her heart. Yes. I remembered Bécquer. But Bécquer . . .

"Bécquer is dead. He died long ago," I said louder than I had intended, my fear, now a wave of panic that threatened to swallow me.

He nodded, nonchalant, a smile playing on his lips as though he was pleased that I remembered him. "In eighteen seventy to be exact. Only, I didn't really die. I just stopped being human."

"And what are you now, then? A monster?"

He winced as if my words had offended him. "I'm not a monster, Carla. I assure you I'm not evil. The change gives us powers, but doesn't alter our true nature. I'm still who I was when I was human. Neither angel, nor demon, but a little bit of both at once."

He had moved to my side as he spoke, and lifting my chair, set it on its legs.

I took a step back. "Don't touch me."

He bowed to me in a formal way that didn't seem out of place. "Would you please sit down?"

I did as he said, mesmerized by his stare and the utter impossibility of his existence.

"You need a drink," he said. "Just wait, I'll bring you one."

Skillfully skirting the tables and the people sitting, eerily still, he walked to the counter where a barista stood, a cup in her frozen hands.

I considered running away, but dismissed the idea as he would find me, I had no doubt, and bring me back. Besides, I wanted answers.

So I waited, my body shaking, until Bécquer came back and, retrieving the contract, set a steaming espresso in front of me.

"I meant to bring you something stronger," he told me, "but couldn't. After twenty years in the States, I still forget they don't always serve alcohol in the cafés here."

"Twenty years? Two more than me."

"I know."

His answer reminded me he had checked me online and thus knew more about me than I would have liked. Not to mention the fact that I had probably given him my card at the conference and so he had my address. Not a reassuring thought.

He motioned for me to drink the coffee. But I could not.

"What do you want of me?"

"Only the honor of editing your work and representing it."

I scowled. "If you were who you claim to be, you'd write your own stories, not waste your time editing mine."

"I'm that Bécquer," he insisted, his eyes dark and serious. "Or I was when I was human." There was anger in his voice and something else, frustration perhaps—or was it pain? "My mind was full of stories then, stories I could easily dress in words to show the world. But since I became an immortal, I have no stories or, if I do, words fail me when I try to capture them. Since I became immortal, I can't write anymore, and I miss it. I miss it terribly. I miss the raw, unrestrained outburst of the artistic creation."

"'When I cannot see words curling like rings of smoke 'round me, I am in darkness—I am nothing,'" I said.

"Virginia Woolf," Bécquer attributed my quote. "My thoughts exactly. That is why I need you. You and others like you who have the gift, so I can bear witness to the birth of their stories and, through them, through their words, feel the flame that now eludes me."

"And that is all you want from me?"

"That is all, I promise."

"Why did you stop time then? Because you did it, right? You can change it back?"

He laughed, amused, it seemed, at the panic I couldn't conceal from my voice as the thought struck me that this was to be forever, that we were to be the only ones alive in a frozen world.

"Yes, I did this, and we will join them in normal time after you give me your answer."

"But I don't understand. Why did you do it?"

"Because of her." He pointed again at the woman by the door. "I was afraid of your reaction were you to learn from Beatriz that I am—immortal."

"Why would she want to tell me?"

"To break your trust in me." He shrugged when I frowned at him. "She's jealous of you because she thinks I want you to take her place."

"As your secretary? Why would I want to?"

"Precisely."

"Didn't you tell her?"

"Of course I did. Yet, she is here. But enough about her. Would you sign with me?"

My thoughts running wild at the idea of Bécquer still being alive, I hesitated.

"If you do," he insisted, "you will never have to worry about the business part of writing. You will be free to write full-time while I deal with the editors and publishers. I used to be terrible at convincing people to buy my stories when I was human, but I'm surprisingly good at it now."

I suppressed a smile. Was he really that clueless or was he just playing me?

Considering his striking features and the fact that most people in the industry were women, I didn't find his success surprising at all. And his offer was most tempting. Like his human self, I also lacked the social skills needed to sell my work. Four months had already passed since I'd started my sabbatical. Four months I had spent mostly querying. If I signed with him, I could maybe finish my sequel before returning to my teaching. Yet . . .

"You're scared of me."

"I—"

Bécquer smiled. "It's only normal. No need to apologize. To fear the unknown is a survival skill we all possess. Would you sign if I promise you I won't hurt anyone?"

I opened my mouth to say no, but didn't. Instead, I nodded.

Bécquer beamed. "Then it's done, for you have my word."

He moved aside the espresso I hadn't touched and once more set the contract in front of me.

"Should I sign with blood?"

A glint of red flashed through his eyes.

"That would be lovely."

I winced.

"But not necessary." He smiled a crooked smile, and passed me a pen, an antique black pen, I swear wasn't there when I asked.

Our fingers brushed as I took it. His were not cold as I imagined, but pleasantly warm, as human's would be.

"I told you I'm not a monster."

With a flourish of his wrist, he signed his name beside mine.

"I will ask Beatriz to send you a copy," he said, whisking the contract into his briefcase.

I looked up at the woman standing by the door and, as I did, she came to life and stepped inside.

With the feline grace that characterized all his movements, Bécquer stood—the noise of his chair skidding on the floor lost in the clamor of conversations that once again filled the room—and motioned his secretary to join us.

"Beatriz," he called, as she came closer, "what a pleasant surprise. We were just talking about you."

He flashed her a smile that would have charmed a miser out of his gold. But the pinched expression on the woman's face remained unchanged. "Indeed," she said and stared at me.

I rose to face her.

"Federico called," Beatriz said after Bécquer had introduced us and told her I had signed with him. "He'll be landing in Philadelphia in an hour and wants you to pick him up."

Bécquer swore with an old-fashioned Spanish word I had never heard spoken. "Why didn't you send Matt?"

"I did. But he insisted he wanted you to go."

Like a boy told he must do his homework before playing, Bécquer sulked. "Is that why you came? To tell me this?"

Beatriz nodded. "I called your cell first. But, as usual, you left it at home."

"I don't need a cell phone."

"You better go," Beatriz insisted. "It took me a while to find you. Federico's plane will be landing soon. And he hates waiting."

"Yes, he does, doesn't he? Even more than he hates me."

"Federico doesn't hate you." Beatriz's voice was firm as if talking to a stubborn child. "He—"

"Then why does he do this to me? Now, I won't have time to arrange things for the party."

Beatriz took a step back as if urging him to follow. "You don't have to worry about that. I told Matt to set the lights and decorations after you left this morning, and I double-checked with the catering service. I thought you were too busy this year to care for such trivial matters."

Bécquer stared her down. "I appreciate your concern," he told her, the stiffness of his body saying otherwise. "But you know I like to attend to the preparations in person."

"You can always change the decorations if they are not to

your liking."

"Of course." He looked at his watch, a flash of gold on his wrist. When he continued, the anger was gone from his voice, "But you were right in asking Matt to do it. If I am to get Federico, I will just make it in time before the first guests arrive. Which reminds me." He turned toward me. "I have not invited you yet. Have I?"

"No, I don't think you have."

"How rude of me! I host a party for my authors and publishers every year for Halloween. I would be thrilled if you came."

"Thank you for the invitation, but—"

"The party starts at six," he interrupted me. "Don't worry about the directions. I'll send Matt to pick you up. Expect him around five-thirty." Then again, he addressed Beatriz. "Please remind him if I forget."

"One more thing," he said to me. "Please, don't mention my— condition. My other authors do not know."

He smiled when I agreed and, after grabbing his briefcase, wrapped one arm around Beatriz's waist and whisked her away.

I watched them go —he, dark and tall, she swaying slightly on her high heels—their closeness bothering me in a way that it shouldn't have.

When they reached the door, he opened it for her with his free hand, his other never leaving her waist, and as she stepped outside, their bodies touched.

Beatriz looked back over her shoulder and glared at me, her pale blue eyes slits of cold hate, her lips closed in a tight line. Then she was gone.

I sat back.

I was breathing hard, I noticed, and my heart was beating fast. What had just happened? Was Beatriz jealous of me, as Bécquer had suggested, jealous that I'd take her place? Or was she warning me that Bécquer was hers? But he wasn't, was he?

"She's my personal secretary," Bécquer had told me. How

personal? I wondered now. Had he meant that they were lovers? And what if they were? Why should that bother me? But they were not, could not be for she was close to my age and he was . . . almost 200 years old.

I closed my eyes for a moment to calm myself. What was I thinking, worrying about Bécquer's private life instead of worrying that he had a life at all, as he, by all logic, should have been long dead? Unless none of this had happened. Unless I had imagined he'd stopped time for us. Unless his claim that he was Bécquer had been a lie.

Outside the window, coming down Main, a blue BMW convertible waited at the light. While I watched, the roof rolled back and the sun poured inside the car, on the black hair and pale skin of the man who claimed to be Bécquer. I held my breath, afraid that he would burst into flames. Across the distance, Bécquer smiled and, in my head, I heard his laughter, a clear laughter of childish joy. Before I could react, the light turned green. With a slight movement of his hand, he shifted gears and disappeared in a blur of blue.

His acknowledgment of my reaction did nothing to assuage my fear because, as far as I was from the window, no human eye could have seen me. And so I knew that Bécquer was Bécquer as he claimed, an immortal that could step out of time, and I, by signing the contract, had just bound myself to him.

I took a deep breath. The smell of coffee now overpowered the other scent, lemon with a hint of cinnamon, that Bécquer had left.

Steam still rose from the second espresso he had brought me. I picked it up and swallowed the coffee in one gulp, burning my tongue. But caffeine did not change how I felt. The fear remained.

Unfortunately, as Bécquer had mentioned, in the States, you can't get brandy in a café. And that was what I needed now, a shot of brandy in my coffee. Or, even better, a shot of brandy straight. I needed a drink.

Chapter Two: Madison

"Good for you!" was all Madison said when I told her I had an agent.

Her headphones back in her ears, she resumed her typing, while talking simultaneously to the heads of her girlfriends trapped on the screen.

"He invited me to his party," I said.

Not surprisingly, I got no answer.

"MA-DI-SON!"

"What?"

"Close your laptop and look at me. We have to talk."

"About what?"

I just stared.

"I have to go," Madison spoke to her laptop, and then snapped it closed. "I was busy," she said, pulling off her headphones.

I ignored the challenge in her voice. For all her attitude, and unlike her brother at her age, she at least obeyed me. For the moment that was enough.

"Have you decided whether you're going to your party tonight?"

"Yes."

"Yes, you have decided, or yes you're going?"

"Yes, as in 'I need a ride to the mall to buy a costume.'"

"Today?"

"It's your fault, or have you forgotten you won't let me wear the one I have?"

"I can't take you to the mall. My party is at six."

"You're going to a party?"

Her surprised disbelief irked me, for it implied this was as rare an event as finding her in a good mood. Which was, in fact, the case.

"Yes, I am. I just told you. My agent invited me."

"Then, you're the one who needs to go to shopping. You have no costume."

"It is not a costume party." I frowned. "At least I don't think it is."

"You don't know? Really Mom, you need help."

"Okay. I'll take you to the mall. You're right. I need a dress."

"Cool!"

Madison jumped from her bed and, in one of those sudden changes of mood I could never predict, sauntered over the piles of clothes scattered on the floor and hugged me. "I love you, you know?" she said.

"Yes, I know."

"Now, about tonight," I said as she started digging into her closet. "I will ask your brother to give you a ride at eight."

Holding a pair of jeans small enough to fit a Barbie doll, she turned to me. "Are you kidding? He'll be too stoned by then to drive."

"Madison! Ryan has been clean for a year."

"If you say so. But if you don't mind, I'd rather ask Abby if her mom can drive us."

I left her texting on her cell, and headed for my room. But her words about Ryan haunted me. Was she badmouthing her brother out of jealousy for all the attention he had gotten over the years by misbehaving, or had she seen something I'd missed?

But what? His urine tests, taken randomly since moving back in with us in late August, had been negative. And, as far as I knew, he had been attending his classes at the community college. A friend of mine taught there and I'd asked her to keep an eye on him. She would have called me had he missed too many classes.

As for his behavior, Ryan was polite to me, as polite as a teenager could be, and whenever he didn't come home to sleep, he always let me know in advance. What else could I do? He was eighteen. I couldn't tie him to a chair. That would be illegal, as the humorless psychologist had told me when I suggested it the previous year. The psychologist my ex had hired to evaluate us and advise the court on who should have custody of Ryan. I had meant it as a joke. He hadn't.

I heard doors opening and closing and the water running in the shower. Drawn by fear and by the memory of a time when this was routine for me—the time last year, when I was trying to find proof that Ryan was using to force my reluctant ex to believe me—I stole into his room.

An unmade bed, a guitar against the wall, open books by the computer, and dirty clothes on the floor. Nothing obvious at first sight suggested drugs. No empty pens, no folded pieces of aluminum foil, and no dryer sheets. None of the paraphernalia I had found then, for at his worst, Ryan had not even tried to hide the evidence, as if he was too wasted to care, or maybe, on a subconscious level, crying for help.

No, nothing obvious, and I had become an expert at detecting everyday objects that could have another, lethal use, or unusual ones, like the glass container I was told was a bong by my friends at Because I Love You, the support group for parents like me. The glass container that, otherwise, I would have put on my mantelpiece. For it had that artsy look.

I bent down and picked up his rumpled jeans. With expert fingers, I checked his pockets: his cell phone as was expected, a box of matches from a club I memorized and, at the very bottom, a small piece of paper, rolled in itself.

I unrolled it distracted, my mind a thousand miles away, already considering what this meant, and the few possibilities I had to make it right, now that Ryan was eighteen. I held the paper in my hand. A business card, I noticed. Then I saw the name, Bécquer's name, beautifully rendered in the old-fashioned calligraphy I had seen earlier today. Bécquer's name yelling at me.

"Ma, what are you doing?"

Lost in my thoughts, I hadn't noticed the water in the shower had stopped running. But it had, and now Ryan stood at the door, a towel wrapped around his waist. The boy who once had fit so snugly in my arms, a boy no more, loomed over me, his dark brows raised in a question.

He wasn't angry. Not yet. Only curious. He wasn't angry, until I raised my hand and showed him the card. "Who gave you this?"

Fast and furious, Ryan reached forward and tore the card from my fingers. "What does it matter?" he asked as he squeezed it in his fist. "Are you spying on me?

"You don't trust me, do you?" he continued, his voice getting louder with each word. "I did what you asked me, I took your dumb tests, and still you don't trust me?"

"Have you met Bécquer?"

"Why should I tell you anything? You won't believe me, anyway."

Before I could answer, he grabbed some clothes from the floor and left the room.

I sat on the bed.

My two worlds that until then I had kept apart, my writing and Ryan's addiction, had unexpectedly collided and lay broken at my feet.

Was Ryan using again? Why had Bécquer not mentioned he knew him?

Could it be he had met him, but didn't know he was my son? Besides, even if Bécquer knew who Ryan was and had given him his card, that didn't mean they had been together when Ryan . . . It was only a rolled card. It didn't have to mean he had been using. But if he hadn't, why had he refused to answer me?

"Mom?" I looked up. Madison, dressed to kill in a short dress over tight pants, and wearing more make-up than I use in a month, stared at me. "Are you ready?"

"Ready?"

Madison pouted. "Don't tell me you're bailing on me? Whatever Ryan has done this time, we need to go to the mall."

Lucky for me, I had somebody to set my priorities straight.

I knew better than to say that aloud, as Madison didn't take well to sarcasm. Besides, she was right, we did need to go to the mall. As things stood between Ryan and me and, despite the fact that Bécquer was not quite human and I barely knew him, my guess was I had a better chance to get an explanation from Bécquer than from my son. And that meant I had to go to the party to talk to him, and thus needed a dress.

I stood up. "No. I'm not bailing on you."

Chapter Three: Federico

Madison rolled her eyes when I pulled the black lace dress from the rack.

"That won't do, Mom. It's Halloween. It has to be a costume party. Why don't you call and ask."

But I couldn't call because I didn't have Bécquer's number with me. Thinking wearing no costume to a costume party would be less embarrassing than to show up in disguise to a regular one, I ignored Madison's advice and bought the dress.

The dress was too fancy for me and much too expensive, but we didn't have time to shop any longer. As it was I had barely finished my make-up when the doorbell rang.

I called to Madison to open the door while I put on my earrings and struggled with the clasp on my necklace.

Downstairs, I could hear a male voice pronouncing my name with a Spanish accent that mimicked mine.

"Mom," Madison called as I left my room. Without inviting the man inside, she climbed the stairs. "I told you it was a costume party," she whispered when she reached me.

I looked over her shoulder at the man framed in the doorway. He was dressed in an ivory suit that would have been in fashion a century before. Yet, by the easy way he carried it off, the jacket open, revealing a white shirt with the two first buttons undone, and a red handkerchief loosely tied around his neck, I knew it was not a costume. I also knew, by the wide smile spread across his face, he had heard Madison's comment.

I smiled back at him. Apologizing would have made the situation even more awkward. Instead, I offered him my hand.

"I'm Carla, and you must be Matt."

He was handsome, I noticed, with black hair and dark sensitive eyes that stared openly at me.

"Federico, actually," he said and took my hand.

I looked at him with renewed interest. Federico. The friend Bécquer didn't want to pick up. The one who didn't want to rent a car.

Federico took a step back. "Shall we?"

In the dim light of the only lamp outside, I noticed a reddish glow in his eyes, a reddish glow that could only mean he was an immortal.

I stopped. Why had I agreed to go to this party? What if immortals fed on human blood like the vampires of lore and the party was Bécquer's excuse to lure me to his house?

But that was absurd. Bécquer had given me his word that he would not harm me. Besides he needed me alive if I was to write for him. And I would not be the only human there. He had invited other authors "who didn't know of his condition," as he had put it. Other authors who had been his clients for years—I had checked—and who were still very much alive. And Beatriz, his secretary, was human too and would be at the party as well. Although this last fact was not reassuring. The hate in her eyes when leaving Café Vienna had been unmistakable. Beatriz would not help me if her boss decided to drink my blood.

I hesitated at the unsetting thought and considered excusing myself. But when I met Federico's eyes, I couldn't bring myself to lie. Besides, I needed to see Bécquer. I needed to ask him why and when he had given his business card to Ryan. So I nodded, put on my coat, and followed Federico into the gathering dusk.

"I really appreciate your picking me up," I told him as we reached the silver Mercedes parked by the curb.

"My pleasure," he said opening the passenger seat for me. "Actually, I'm in your debt. Bécquer and Beatriz were arguing and I was glad to have an excuse to leave the house."

"Why were they arguing?" I asked him after we joined the traffic.

Federico stole a quick glance at me, as if wondering how much

I knew, then shrugged. "The usual," he said. Without warning he switched to Spanish, his words flowing fast, in the clipped pattern of Southern Spain. "As far as I can tell, she didn't want Bécquer to represent your work."

"Why not?"

"I wouldn't be offended if I were you," he continued, without answering my question. "On the contrary. Beatriz has no literary talent. Yet she has taken it upon herself to save humanity. Through books. She believes only philosophy treatises should be published, and literary books dealing with the human condition. You know the ones where nothing happens and the authors are so much in love with their own writing, they forget to tell a story. I don't understand why Bécquer has put up with her this long."

"You don't like her much."

"The feeling is mutual."

"That wasn't my impression. This morning, she convinced Bécquer to go to the airport to pick you up."

He braked sharply and swerved off the road, bringing the car to a halt on the dirt shoulder.

"Bécquer didn't want to go?"

"He . . . he had things to do and—"

"Things to do. Like what? Decorating the house? I haven't seen him in a year, and he needs convincing?"

His voice rose as he spoke so that by now he was shouting.

I looked ahead at the trees caught in the headlights and waited for his anger to pass. When he spoke again, he sounded subdued.

"What else did he say about me?" he asked.

"Nothing. Really. He left right after Beatriz came. Well, not after she came. First, he stopped time for us so she wouldn't interfere with my signing the contract."

"He stopped time? So you know? You know what—who he is?"

I nodded.

"What about me? Did he tell you who I am?"

"No, he didn't mention it."

"Of course not. I'm not important enough. For two decades we were lovers. And what am I to him now? An inconvenience when I come to visit, an errand to add to his list of things to do before his guests arrive."

I gasped. Lovers? Bécquer and Federico were—had been lovers?

Federico was not looking at me, but straight ahead, his hands grabbing the wheel with such intensity it broke loose. He stared at it for a moment as if puzzled, then opening the door, threw it against the darkness. His eyes flaring red, he turned to me.

He hates me, Bécquer had said. *He doesn't,* Beatriz had told him. And she was right. Federico didn't hate Bécquer. He was in love with him.

I stood still, eerily aware I was sitting next to a man who was not human and that, for all his gentle appearance, could break my neck without even trying. As he had the wheel.

I had to leave. Now.

My hand trembling uncontrollably, I reached for the door.

"Don't." Federico's arm flashed in front of me and grabbed my hand.

"Please, don't," he repeated, his voice softer now, apologetic. "Bécquer might forgive me for breaking his car. Or for failing to drive you to the party. But if I do both, he will kill me for sure."

I frowned, surprised at his self-deprecating tone. "I thought you were immortal."

"I'm sure he would find a way," Federico said, releasing my hand. "His ingenuity to cause me pain knows no limit."

"You love him."

I regretted my words the moment I said them for I was afraid my inappropriate comment would throw him into another fit of anger. But Federico didn't seem to hear. He was staring at the gaping hole in the dashboard where the wheel used to be as if willing another one to appear.

"Bécquer is right," he said after a moment. "I do overreact sometimes."

He sounded so defeated I felt sorry for him. Bécquer was charming, I had to admit. It was not difficult for me to imagine falling for him and the pain at his rejection.

"Not at all," I agreed to keep him calm. "Your reaction was understandable given the circumstances. He should have offered to pick you up."

"You think?"

When I nodded, he added wistfully, "Let's hope Bécquer agrees with you when I tell him."

I waited for him to produce a phone and call Bécquer to ask him to give us a ride. Although it wasn't cold outside, I was not looking forward to walking in my too tight black dress and fancy shoes. But Federico didn't move and when, after digging into my handbag, I offered him mine, he shook his head.

"That won't be necessary. Bécquer just told me Matt is coming."

"He told you? But how? You didn't . . ." I waved my phone at him.

Federico shrugged. "I don't need a phone to talk with Bécquer when we are this close."

"You can read his mind?"

"Not exactly. I only hear what he wants to share. I cannot force myself into his mind. He would notice and block me. Actually, he just did that before, when—Did Bécquer ask you to be his . . . secretary?"

"No, why would I want to be his secretary? I'm a writer."

"Of course." He smiled, a friendly smile that lit a twinkle of mischief in his eyes. And I found myself warming to him. "And what do you write, if I may ask?"

"Fantasy stories set in medieval times."

"It sounds like something Bécquer would love, and Beatriz would hate."

"And you?"

"Me? I would have to read the story first. I used to write dramas when I was human. But I've mellowed with time."

"You were a writer before you were immortal?"

"I was indeed."

Federico bent forward and worked the CD player with his long fingers until he found the right track. "Listen," he said. Sitting back against his seat, he closed his eyes.

The broken voice of Leonard Cohen came through the speakers, declaiming a poem-made-song. The first song I had danced to at my wedding with the husband who had since become a stranger: *Take This Waltz.*

Federico, eyes still closed, sang along, keeping the beat on the dashboard with his fingers.

I looked at him in profile and, as if seeing him for the first time, I noticed his dark wavy hair, his cleft chin, and his arched bushy eyebrows. I gasped. "You are Federico."

My voice broke before I could complete his full name: Federico García Lorca, the most beloved Spanish poet in the twentieth century.

Federico nodded. "Yes. I am 'that' Federico."

Without missing a beat, he resumed his singing, his voice fitting perfectly the lyrics of the song, the lyrics that were Cohen's translation into English of Lorca's perfect words.

Chapter Four: Matt

"My cross, indeed," Federico said when the song ended, repeating the last words of the poem. "I wrote this years before I met Bécquer and he made me an immortal. I wrote it for a lover long forgotten. But they reflect my feelings for Bécquer exactly, on our first winter in Vienna."

"Bécquer made you an immortal?"

Federico nodded.

"Why? Did you ask him to do it?"

"No. I was unconscious when he found me, bleeding through my broken skull and half buried in the ditch that was meant to be my grave. I didn't ask him to do it, but I don't blame him. I would have died otherwise.

"I don't blame him either for my falling for him. He never claimed that he loved me. Never hid his other lovers from me, the ladies he lured with his charm and forgot as soon as they loved him, for it was his gift that they would love him, his curse that he could not love them back, after they fell for him."

"He played with them, and with you. Why did you let him?"

Federico shook his head. "He didn't play with me. I knew he didn't love me. He couldn't, nor the way I wanted: Bécquer is not gay. He took me as his lover to heal my broken soul when he realized I did not want to live. I had lost my will to live that summer of 1936 when I witnessed my friends betray me and saw the void of undiluted hate in the eyes of my killers.

"Bécquer cured me of my despair. He took me as his lover and healed my soul with his passion and words of love he reinvented for me. I fell in love with him, how could I not? But he never guessed it. He had not planned or expected this to happen. Until he met me, he thought immortals could not love.

"When I told him, when he realized how much he meant to me, how much I hurt when I saw him with others, he left me, making clear that, from then on, I was allowed to see him only once a year for a week. He thought, that way, I would forget him."

"But you did not."

Federico stared at me. "Don't let his charm blind you, Carla. Do not fall for him."

I laughed, too eagerly perhaps. "I won't, don't worry. Bécquer's only my agent."

"Of course."

Turning his head away from me, Federico looked through the window to the road ahead. "Matt is coming," he said. "Good. I was starting to suspect Bécquer had forgotten to pass him my message."

I followed his stare, and saw nothing but a wall of darkness beyond the halo of our headlights.

"Don't worry. He'll be here soon. I feel his mind."

"You feel his mind? So Matt is an immortal too?"

"Not at all. Matt is quite human."

"But . . . then. Are you saying you can read minds? Human minds?"

"No. I don't read minds. I sense them when they are close enough."

He said it casually as if unaware of the magnitude of what he had just revealed to me.

"You tricked me, didn't you? Right now. When you asked me about Bécquer, you forced me to think of him so you could read my feelings for him."

"Yes."

"How dare you?"

"I needed to know to warn you that Bécquer . . . " He stopped and with a sudden movement of his hand flashed the headlights. As if conjured by his signal, a beam of light glowed in the distance. "Matt is almost here. I'll explain later, I promise, after we change cars."

He was still speaking when a car drew near and, leaving the road, came to a stop facing us. It was not the blue convertible Bécquer had driven in the morning, but a white limousine. Somehow, the idea that Bécquer owned still another car—Federico had told me the silver Mercedes was Bécquer's also—irked me in an irrational way I found most disturbing.

"Carla?"

I turned toward Federico's voice and found him standing outside the car, holding the door open.

Too startled to speak, as I had no recollection of him leaving my side, I took his hand and stepped outside. Beyond the halo of the limousine, I saw a man emerge from the driver's seat.

With easy strides, Federico walked toward him. "Hi, Matt," he greeted him, as he got closer. "So nice of you to come."

"My pleasure, as always," the man said, in a formal way that belied his age. For he was young, I realized once I moved into the beam's halo and the light stopped blinding me. His youth made even more evident because, instead of the standard suit I had expected, he was wearing a leather jacket and tight black jeans with metal chains hanging from his belt.

"Nice costume."

Matt sulked. "I thought all the guests had arrived so I had already changed when Mr. Bécquer asked me to come at once. Please, Don Federico, don't tell my mother I came like this."

"Don't worry, I won't mention your costume to her, you have my word."

Matt smiled a crooked smile that lit his face with pride. "It's not a costume. I'm playing later."

Federico raised an eyebrow in mock admiration. "A paying gig?"

Matt nodded.

"My congratulations," Federico said, taking the boy's hand in both of his and shaking it firmly.

Matt shivered at the contact, and when Federico moved toward the car, Matt's eyes followed him. If Federico noticed the boy's reaction—how could he not when he could sense feelings?—he said nothing.

I didn't mention it either when we were sitting side by side in the back of the car, although the window to the front seat was closed and Matt could not hear us. The boy's feelings for Federico were none of my business, and I was still upset at Federico for intruding on the privacy of my mind.

"How many cars does Bécquer have?" I asked him instead.

Federico frowned. "Two that I know of. This limo is not his. He rented it for the party. But why do you care?"

"I don't."

"Yes. Bécquer is quite wealthy." Federico answered the question I had not asked. "When you can manipulate minds to do your bidding, it is not surprising the books you represent end up on the bestseller list. Money follows."

"Manipulate minds? Is that what you are doing with me?"

"No. I have never manipulated anybody's mind." I glowered at him. "I'm afraid you'd have to take my word for it," he insisted. "I cannot prove it to you."

"But Bécquer does—manipulate minds, I mean?"

Federico shrugged. "I don't think he does it on purpose. Every time I have confronted him about it, he has denied it. Yet things seem always to go his way. In business and in love."

"Is that what you wanted to warn me about?"

Federico stared ahead, crossing and uncrossing his fingers as if trying to clarify his thoughts.

"Bécquer has a new love interest," he said at last. "I thought she might be you."

"Me? That's absurd. I only met him twice."

"But he has read your books, liked them enough to sign you as a client. And Bécquer is quite impulsive when falling in love. Childish you may say. He falls not so much for the person but for his own idealized image of her. Seeing you twice would be more than enough for him to think himself fully in love, especially when he has glimpsed your soul in your stories. Yes, you could have been his new beloved. I'm glad to see that you're not."

"And you know that by reading my mind?"

"In a way. For if Bécquer were in love with you, he'd have charmed you already and you'd be blindly in love with him."

"But I wouldn't be really in love with him. My feelings would be an illusion."

"Exactly my point. You wouldn't be yourself anymore, just a puppet to his will. Yet Bécquer doesn't seem to realize that distinction. He insists he does not change the feelings for a first attraction must be there. He just pushes the victim slightly in that direction.

"Victim being my chosen word, of course. The so-called victims would call themselves fortunate, because to be chosen, to be loved by Bécquer, is an exhilarating experience. Nobody, not a single one of them has complained yet and, trust me, he has had many."

"What happens when he tires of them?"

"They still love him for a while, I guess. But when he stops charming them, their love eventually wanes and they forget him, and thus forgive him for leaving them.

"In fact, most of them remain friends with him until he moves on. For, of course, like all immortals, he can't stay more than twenty years in a place before his not aging becomes obvious. Then he has to go somewhere else and reinvent himself."

Twenty years he had told me. He had lived in the States for twenty years. Did that mean he was ready to move? Now that I'd just found an agent, was he about to disappear and leave me agentless once more? He wouldn't, now, would he? That would just be rude.

Federico laughed.

"Are you reading my mind again?"

"I wouldn't if you were not shouting."

"I wasn't."

"Anger sounds that way to me, to us immortals. Don't worry. He's not planning to leave. Not yet. He's been an agent for ten years only."

I sighed in relief. I guess an immortal, manipulative agent was, in my book, better than no agent at all. Which didn't say much about my ethics. Maybe I shouldn't be so harsh on Federico for reading my mind. It was not as if he could help it.

"Friends?" Federico asked.

"Friends."

As I spoke, the car came to a stop. Through the window, I saw the facade of an imposing stone house covered in ghoulish spider webs glistening in the glow of blinking orange lights. Several jack-o'-lanterns flickered on the stairs that led to the porch.

"Oh well, here we are," Federico said. "Let's hope I'm wrong because if Bécquer is in love, Beatriz is going to cause him trouble."

"Beatriz?"

"Forget what I just said, and let's go inside and enjoy ourselves. Bécquer's parties are always interesting. I have the impression this one will not disappoint."

Chapter Five: The Portrait

Matt opened the limousine door for me. Although I didn't delay, by the time I got out, Federico was already coming around the front of the car, the gravel crackling under his light steps.

"Thank you," he said to the young man. "Please don't forget to call the garage and ask them to tow the Mercedes."

"I have already."

Federico smiled. "Great. Now you better park this one in the back before your mother sees you."

Matt glanced toward the house. "I better," he agreed and, with a nod in my direction and a last longing stare at Federico, he disappeared inside the car.

Federico waved his hand toward the house and motioned me to go first.

Following his suggestion, I crossed the open space and climbed the stairs.

Up close the spider webs looked too perfect to be spooky and the artistic designs in the jack-o'-lanterns flanking the stairs to the porch inspired more awe than fear. An aged iron ring hung on the right side of the massive double doors that would have been perfectly in place at a Castilian noble house.

Just as Federico reached my side, the doors swung open and a woman appeared in the doorway. A woman dressed in a low cut dress with a tight bodice and a long skirt that fell to the floor.

"Here you are at last," she said as a way of hello.

Her face was in shadow, but her voice, I recognized. It was Beatriz's. Beatriz, wearing a dress that belonged to the mid-nineteenth century, to the time in which Bécquer had been human. Madison had been right, I realized with regret: this was a costume party.

"What a perfect choice." Federico's voice broke through my thoughts. "Bécquer must be delighted that you honor him so."

I looked up, puzzled by Federico's words. Tossing back her auburn hair that fell in waves over her shoulders, Beatriz revealed a silk blue scarf.

"*La banda azul,*" I whispered.

The blue scarf that Beatriz, the protagonist of one of Bécquer's most beloved short stories, loses in the mountains. The blue scarf she goads her cousin to go find later that evening. He agrees because he loves her but does so against his best judgment for it's Halloween and, that night, the mountains are said to be haunted by the souls of dead warriors that roam the earth trapped in their skeletal bodies. The following morning, Beatriz finds the scarf torn and bloody in her room and dies of fright guessing right that her cousin never returned from his quest alive.

Beatriz smiled. "So you noticed."

I saw a glint of victory in her eyes as they moved up and down my embarrassingly plain, black dress. "Please, come in," she said and moved back. "Bécquer is waiting for you."

I breathed deeply to ease my discomfort, and was about to follow her when I felt the pull of Federico's hand on my arm.

"Thank you, Beatriz," Federico said. "But Carla and I are not quite ready yet. Don't worry about Bécquer. You are so lovely tonight, I'm sure you can charm him into forgetting everybody else."

Beatriz stared at Federico, like a tiger about to jump its prey. But Federico stared her down. "Of course," she said, and closed the door, leaving us standing outside.

Federico smiled when I frowned at him. "I apologize. I should have realized that this being a costume party, you would feel uncomfortable not wearing one. Please, come with me."

I hesitated. "Don't you think it is a little too late now to go get a costume?"

"Don't worry. We don't have to go anywhere. A mask will do.

And I know where to find one."

I followed Federico around the porch decorated with white ghosts and black witches' hats until he reached another door set on the left aisle of the L-shaped building.

"Are you sure Bécquer doesn't want you to be his secretary?" he asked me as we walked.

"I told you I'm a writer. And, I assure you that organization is not one of my assets. No one would hire me as secretary. Why?"

"Because Beatriz thinks so and resents you."

"Did you sense that in her?"

"No. I cannot sense Beatriz. I know because she conveniently forgot to tell you about the costume."

"You can't read her? But she is human."

We had reached the end of the porch and Federico stopped by a side door. "It depends whom you ask," he said as he turned the knob. "Matt is not so sure."

"Matt?"

"Yes, Matt. From what he tells me, she is not the maternal type." When I looked at him nonplussed, he added, "Beatriz is Matt's mother."

He smiled at my surprise and motioned me inside. We left our coats and my purse on the iron rack set against the wall, and then climbed the stairs to the second floor.

Crossing the door at the end of the corridor, we entered a big room furnished with a low table, a love seat with silver leaves on dark blue velvet, and an antique desk set before matching curtains that, I guessed, covered windows.

Federico asked me to wait there and disappeared, through a set of French doors. From where I stood I could see that the next room was even larger and was dominated by a four-poster bed carved from dark wood. Several pillows were arranged on top of the blue eiderdown. Both the bed and the heavy wooden chest with iron reinforcements that sat at its foot were of Castilian style. That and the familiar smell of lemon and cinnamon that permeated the air made me realize this was, most probably, Bécquer's bedroom.

Startled at the thought that I was intruding on his privacy, I stepped back and bumped hard against the low table behind me. I swore under my breath at the sudden pain in my leg, and then again at the thump of metal hitting on wood.

I turned.

Two picture frames lay face down on the table. I picked one up. It was an oval painting of three children, the eldest one formally dressed in an old-fashioned suit, the two little ones in white gowns. A boy and two girls. Or maybe three boys, I corrected myself, as I remembered young boys used to wear gowns in centuries past. I set the painting back down and took the other frame. It was a photograph, a color picture of a young man I knew well. A picture of my son.

I started, my thoughts reeling in confusion. Why did Bécquer have a picture of my boy? And not just a picture among many, a collage of faces tacked to a cork, the way Madison kept the pictures of her friends. But an 8-by-10. A picture taken with care, framed with love. Love. The word brought to my mind Federico's conversation in the car, his conviction that despite his denial, Bécquer had a new lover.

At the disturbing image my mind had conjured, my hands froze and the picture slid through my fingers and hit the wooden floor. This time the glass shattered.

The sound broke my reverie. I shook my head. What was wrong with me? The boy could not be Ryan, just someone who resembled him. I kneeled and lifted the picture. Over a dozen straight lines diverged from a central breaking point making recognition impossible. Holding the frame in my shaking hands, I removed the bigger piece of broken glass to uncover the boy's face.

It was Ryan. No doubt about it. Ryan smiling as he had not done at me in a long time.

I swore in anger and disgust. Anger at Bécquer for stealing my son, disgust because he had charmed him with his powers, for I knew Ryan was not gay. I had seen him fall in love when he was barely two at the sight of a beautiful girl dressed all in black. I had seen his head turn 180 degrees to follow a pretty neighbor in a too-short skirt a couple of years ago. No, Ryan was not gay.

"Carla," Federico's voice called from the door.

I stood. Holding Ryan's picture in front of me, like a priest would hold a cross to exorcise a demon. I advanced toward him. "Since when?" I demanded, my voice raw with hate.

Federico's look of concern quickly changed to alarm as his eyes fell on my hands. "Stop," he ordered. His voice, low but firm, entered my mind, overpowering my will. I stopped.

"Please, Carla, put it down. Whatever it is that has upset you, we can talk about it in a civilized way."

The pressure in my mind had dwindled to almost bearable limits, as his tone changed from commanding to pleading. I didn't move.

"Put. It. Down."

Again his voice resonated in my head with an intensity that erased any resistance. Powerless I saw my hands moving, as if they didn't belong to me.

"On the floor."

I set the picture down.

"The glass." Federico's words burned bright red inside my head.

Confused, I hesitated for a moment. Then I noticed the piece of glass I still held in my right hand and bent again.

With a speed that was not human—as if I needed a reminder of that unsettling fact—Federico was at my side and, lifting me by the waist, pushed me against the wall.

"Why did you try to kill me?"

I felt the pressure of his mind on mine. A pressure that turned to pain so that it made thinking impossible. Or lying.

I shook my head. "I didn't." Even in my ears my voice sounded weak. "I did not try to kill you. How could I?"

"Don't lie to me. Remember I can read your feelings. And there was murder in your mind."

"Bécquer—I was thinking of Bécquer. Not you."

His eyes, glowing red, stayed on mine but, as the pressure in my mind eased and disappeared, Federico set me on the floor and took a step back. "Why? Why do you hate Bécquer? What caused the sudden change?"

Too shaken to explain, I pointed at the frame lying on the floor.

Again Federico moved almost too fast for me to see. When he came back the picture was in his hands. "Do you know this boy?"

"He's my son."

Federico gasped. In the silence that followed I could almost hear his mind working along the lines mine had followed.

"You think Bécquer fancies your son," he said at last, voicing my assumption. "You think they're lovers. That is why you're angry at him."

I nodded. "What other explanation is there?"

"Does your son like men?" Unlike mine, Federico's voice was even.

"No. That is why this is so very wrong. Apart from the fact that Ryan is only eighteen and Bécquer is what—two hundred years old? He has forced him. He has charmed him to do his bidding."

Federico shook his head. "I understand your concern, Carla. But I think you're mistaken. Bécquer is not gay. In all the years I have known him, I was his only male lover. And, please believe me, Bécquer would never force anyone."

"That is a lie. You told me so yourself. You told me that he charms his lovers."

"But the attraction must be there. And if your son is not gay—"

"Don't play with me. I know you can control humans. You did it with me right now. You are monsters."

Federico moved back as if I had slapped him. Taking advantage of his hesitation, I ran to the door. But when I reached it, Federico was already there, blocking my exit.

"Carla, please. Wait. There is something you need to see."

His tone was not threatening. It needn't be. "Do I have a choice?"

"I'm afraid not."

Gently but firmly, Federico steered me to the desk set against the far wall. He moved back the chair and, once I was sitting, produced a key—from where, I didn't see—and opened the top drawer.

Careful, almost reverentially, he removed a leather-bound book and set it on the table.

"Open it."

As I did what he ordered, I realized it was not a book, but an album, its thick pages yellowed with age separated by onion sheets. Each page held a photograph of a different boy. As I turned the pages, the pictures, yellowed with age and vignetted around the edges at first, became color prints, and the serious expressions in the boys' faces gave way to playful smiles.

"No," Federico said, reading my mind. "They are not his lovers, but the children he has sponsored over the years."

I looked up.

"How much do you know about Bécquer's life? His human life?"

"I know he died in his thirties. But, of course, he didn't. So I guess I know nothing. Only that he wrote short stories and poems published under the title *Rimas y Leyendas*."

"Which, by the way, were not widely known when he was human. All his life, his human life, Bécquer struggled and failed to be recognized as a writer, but that is another story. What matters here is that Bécquer had three children, three boys. They were young when he died, the oldest barely eight."

"The boys in the frame," I whispered.

Federico frowned as if not following my train of thought. Then nodded. "Yes. That painting is the only thing he has of them. That and his memories.

"Bécquer loved his children more than anything. 'Take care of my children,' he asked his friends shortly before his staged death.

And they did. They published his work the following year, and Bécquer ensured it sold well to procure enough money for his children and his wife. Still, he missed them."

"Couldn't he see them afterward?"

"No. It's forbidden. The Elders, the Immortals Council, if you wish, doesn't allow it.

"That's why to alleviate his longing, he took care of various children over the years. Orphans as Bécquer himself had been since the age of eleven, children with artistic talents, or just children he met who needed help. He gave them a chance at life, but never interfered afterward. There was nothing dark in their relationship, nothing he should be ashamed of. My guess is that Ryan is his latest interest."

"Ryan is not an orphan, and he's eighteen."

"Is he gifted?"

I shrugged. "He's good at music."

Federico lifted the album. "If he's one of them, he must be here." He passed the pages forward, then stopped. I felt his intake of breath, as he slammed it close.

"What is it Federico?"

"Nothing."

"Let me see."

He hesitated for a moment, and then handed it to me. "Please don't jump to conclusions. It's just a picture."

I didn't notice anything unusual at first. Yes, Bécquer was standing close to Ryan, their hands touching. But it made sense in the context as he was directing Ryan's fingers on the strings of the guitar my son was holding.

It was a candid picture, obviously amateurish as the top of Bécquer's head was cut off and neither of them was looking at the camera. Yet it was terribly effective at conveying the easy rapport that existed between them.

"They are close," I said.

"It doesn't mean they are lovers," Federico said. But there was doubt in his voice.

It was only as I turned back the pages to compare the picture of my son with the others, that I noticed the difference: Bécquer was not in them. Bécquer was not in any of them, because his picture would have given away the fact that he didn't age. But then, why had he kept this picture of him and Ryan?

I looked up and met Federico's eyes.

"You are right, Carla, something is different in Bécquer's relationship with Ryan. Still, I don't believe Bécquer has forced him. Please, let me talk with Bécquer. Let me ask him what Ryan is to him. I promise I'll report to you what he tells me."

"No."

I stood to go, but Federico grabbed my arm. "I don't want you to get hurt, Carla. But you must understand, I won't let you hurt Bécquer either."

"As if I could."

"Don't pretend with me."

"Pretend?"

Federico stared at me for a long time and I knew he was reading my feelings and resented him for it, but could do nothing to stop him. Finally, he shook his head. "Either you're good at hiding it or you really don't know."

"Know what?"

"About the glass."

"Know what about the glass?"

"I can't tell you."

"I see. You don't trust me, but I must trust you. I don't think so."

Federico sighed. "You're right. If you are to trust me, I must trust you too. But before I do, promise you won't ever repeat what I'm about to say."

"We call ourselves immortals, but that is a misnomer," Federico told me when I promised. "We can die."

"How?"

"You really don't expect me to answer that, do you? Let's say we heal fast. Any wound we receive disappears almost instantly once the object that caused it is removed. But a cut from glass doesn't close as fast, and the loss of blood leaves us vulnerable."

"You heal fast. How fast are we talking?"

"Let me show you."

From somewhere about his person, he produced a pocketknife. Holding the blade in his right hand, he ran it over his left palm. Briefly, the line he traced filled with blood then closed again, or so it seemed to me for, as I looked, my vision blurred. As my knees gave way, I fell into darkness.

Chapter Six: The Kiss

When I came back to my senses, I was lying on the four-poster bed I had seen through the French doors that opened into Bécquer's room. I tried to sit, but the walls started spinning, so I gave in and laid back once more against the pillows. Through the cotton cloud that filled my mind, I heard angry voices coming from the anteroom. Bécquer's voice and Federico's. Then Bécquer's again, louder this time.

"Why did you bring her here?"

So much for my hope that he never learned I had been in his room. I didn't have to strain my ears to hear Federico's answer for he was also shouting.

"Because you forgot to tell her this was a costume party, and your dear Beatriz didn't waste time to point it out to her. I came to find her a mask."

"What does it matter whether she is wearing a stupid costume or not?"

"It matters to her."

"I see. What would I do without you, Federico? I guess being straight has its disadvantages. I miss those subtleties in women you see so well."

"So you're straight? Still?"

"What kind of question is that? Of course I'm straight."

"Then why did you frame the picture of her son?"

"Ryan." Bécquer's voice was softer now, almost inaudible. "His name is Ryan."

"You love him," Federico shouted. "You love this boy. Don't deny it. I know you too well. Your voice changed when you said his name."

"Yes, I love him. But it is not what you think."

"Stop lying to me, Bécquer. I'm tired of it. You know I'd give my life for you a thousand times. The only thing I ask is that you tell me the truth. And you haven't."

"What are you talking about?"

"I asked you this morning if you had a new lover, and you said you didn't. But it was a lie."

"It wasn't."

"I don't believe you. I think you were ashamed of confessing that you had taken a boy and forced him against his nature. Or maybe not ashamed, maybe he has resisted you. Has he? Is that why you signed Carla, to have an excuse to be close to her son?"

"You're out of your mind."

"I think not. I feared that Beatriz was going to get you in trouble with the Elders. Now I hope she will. The only thing I regret is that I won't be here when it happens because I'm leaving. Now."

"Calm down, Federico. You're overreacting as usual."

"Goodbye, Bécquer."

"Federico!"

I had left the bed upon hearing Federico's accusations and Bécquer's weak denials and, as the door slammed close behind Federico, I slid the French doors open and entered the anteroom.

"Is that true?" I asked to Bécquer's back.

Bécquer turned.

Despite the fury that burned inside me, my breath caught in my chest, for he was a vision of beauty in his three-piece black suit, the jacket open to reveal a white shirt, a red vest, a white rosebud caught in its lapel. His black hair, slightly longer than fashionable, came almost to his shoulders, framing his handsome face that, even now flustered in anger, had the beauty of a Michelangelo statue come to life.

In a swift movement, Bécquer was by my side. "How much have you heard?" he asked, a trace of irritation in his voice.

"Answer me. Is that why you chose me? To be close to my son?"

His eyes glowed red. "No. I chose you because you have the gift. The gift of turning words into stories. The gift and nothing else in a world that is blind to beauty and deaf to song. And thus, you, like me when I was alive, like all of us with an artist's soul, struggle to survive, but not quite make it, for we have no mind for business. That is why I chose you. I thought you needed me. I thought I could be of help to you."

"I may need you, but my son is not the price."

"I agree. He's not. I never meant him to be."

"Then why do you have his picture?"

"Because . . . " For the first time ever, Bécquer struggled for words. "Would you please take a seat, Carla, I—"

"No. Tell me."

He hesitated for a moment longer. "All right." He took a deep breath. "I have his picture because Ryan is my descendant."

"Your what?"

"My descendant. His great grandfather, your grandfather, Carla, was my grandson."

"You expect me to believe that?"

Bécquer shrugged. "It's the truth. I was human once, you know, and I had children."

You're my ancestor was all I could think. This man to whom I was, undeniably attracted, was my ancestor. I started shaking.

"Are you sure you don't want to sit?"

I shook my head. But when he grabbed my arm and guided me to the sofa, I didn't resist.

Bécquer didn't sit, but walked to the curtains that covered the wall and, after drawing them aside, stood by the window, his eyes lost in the distance as if reading a story in the darkness outside. Finally he turned and, pulling out a chair that stood by the desk, dragged it over and sat heavily, facing me.

"All right. Here is the truth. You're a descendant of my wife's third child. But you are not biologically my descendant for the baby was not mine. My wife and I had parted ways more than a year before his birth. She had left me for she loved somebody else.

"When her son was born, I recognized him as mine, out of shame perhaps, or as I wish to believe, out of concern for the baby who would have been shunned otherwise. So, in a way, I didn't lie to you before because legally he was my son and later when he came to live with me, I loved him as such."

The warmth in his voice when he talked betrayed the strength of his feelings. I sighed deeply, relieved to learn he was not my ancestor for his love for this boy—who in that time long ago when he was human had caused him so much shame—had only increased my attraction to him.

"Thank you for telling me."

He shrugged. "Do you believe me now?"

"So you knew about me and my children all these years. Why did you approach Ryan now?"

"No, I didn't know about you until recently. When I became immortal, I had to give up seeing my children. I followed them from afar over the years—my children and their children and their children's children—making sure they were all right.

"Then, for personal reasons, I left Spain in 1936, at the beginning of the Spanish Civil War. When I came back, years later, I couldn't find my descendants anymore. That monstrous war had swallowed them, and erased all trace that I had ever been alive."

"My grandfather died in Madrid the first year of the war," I explained to him. "My grandmother moved north after it ended, with their son, my father. That's why you couldn't find him."

"I know. I ran a search on you." He smiled his disarming smile as I glowered at him. "Don't get upset. I read your book first then got curious about you, a Spaniard whose last name was Esteban. Could it be we were related?"

"But your last name is—"

"Dominguez, actually, not Bécquer. But Emilio took his mother's name, Esteban, when he was of age after he learned the truth about his birth, I guess.

"You are his descendant. I had no doubt," Bécquer continued. "And when I learned you had a son, I had to meet him."

"I have a daughter too."

A fleeting smile played on his lips. "I don't do so well with girls."

I was about to give him some feminist speech about his blatant misogyny when I remembered Madison's moody behavior of late and let it pass. I wasn't doing well with girls these days either.

"How did you meet Ryan?" I asked him instead.

"I arranged to give a talk at his college and approached him afterward. When I discovered he played guitar, I told him to call me for I knew Matt's band was looking for a new member. He called a week later and I invited him to come over to meet Matt."

"You gave him your card?"

Bécquer stared at me. "Probably. Why?"

"I found it in his pocket today."

"He's not using."

"How did you know—?" I stopped as I realized that, like Federico, Bécquer was reading my mind, or whatever it was immortals did. I glared at him.

"Sorry. I didn't mean to intrude."

"Then don't."

He shrugged. "You don't have to worry about Ryan. He's clean. You must be proud of him. It's hard to give up an addiction. Believe me, I know."

He got up. "Now that everything has been clarified between us, let's go. Whether I want it or not, I have a party to host. Which reminds me . . . "

He was gone and back so fast that, but for the mask he held now in his hands, I wouldn't have noticed he had moved at all.

I stood and examined the mask, a delicate piece of art made of ivory silk with colorful feathers.

"Don't you like it?" Bécquer asked, as I hesitated to pick it up.

"It's beautiful."

Again he smiled, the smile of a child pleased with himself. "Federico bought it for me last year when he was in Venice."

He talked about Federico affectionately as if he had already forgotten his friend had just stomped out of the room, threatening to leave at once. When I mentioned this to him, he shook his head. "He won't leave. He's with Matt." And for the way he said it, as a fact, I understood he was feeling his mind. Did he know, I wondered, of Matt's attraction to Federico? But, of course, he must.

"Shouldn't you apologize to him?"

"Apologize to him?" Bécquer repeated, his eyes glowing red. "How can you suggest such a thing? He was the one who insulted me. He accused me of perverting Ryan—"

"Why didn't you tell him the truth?"

"And spoil his fun? Federico enjoys thinking the worst of me."

"That's not true. He worships you."

"I wish he didn't. I am no god. Thus, no matter what I do, he's bound to be disappointed."

"I think you like him to worship you. Or you would have put an end to his infatuation long ago."

"Don't you think I've tried?"

"Obviously not hard enough."

"What is that supposed to mean?"

"Stop playing games with him, Bécquer. If you really want Federico to forget you, you must treat him like your equal. Tell him the truth."

"I will eventually."

"Do it now. Mind to mind."

"Even if I did, he won't believe me because he would sense I'm hiding something from him. Which I am. But what I'm hiding is a surprise for him, not an ugly secret of mine. I'm hiding that I taught Matt and Ryan to play some of his poems set to song, and they're going to perform them tonight.

"So you see why I have the right to be resentful of him? I plan a concert in his honor, and he pays me back by throwing wild accusations at me."

"You care what he thinks," I said, for the eagerness of his discourse suggested he was genuinely hurt.

"You seem surprised. I see. Federico has convinced you that I'm a monster. It's useless. No matter what I do, Federico will never forgive me."

"He has forgiven you long ago. It's forgetting he has trouble with."

Bécquer looked away.

"We must go," he said, "the guests are waiting. And I want you to meet Richard Malick. He's interested in your manuscript."

He offered me his arm, but I hesitated. I don't like parties. Parties are full of people. I like people in small doses. Not all at once. And, if facing a room full of strangers was enough to send me into a panic, talking with a publisher, even if that was the main reason I had come to the party, made my knees grow weak.

"Are you all right?" Bécquer asked.

I breathed in. "Yes."

"You don't seem all right to me. And you just fainted. Why?"

"I . . . Federico cut himself. I can't stand the sight of blood."

Bécquer frowned, and stared at me, his face expressionless, his eyes as dark as unfathomable wells. As I stared back, his lips parted, to reveal white flashing teeth. For a moment, his canines, longer than what seemed normal, rested on his lower lip.

I didn't see him move, yet he must have, because his body was close to mine, his hands cupped my face, and his lips were on my lips, pressing them open. Over the familiar scent of lemon and cinnamon that was his, I felt the salty taste of blood and in my mind I heard his words: "Take it. You must take it."

As he spoke, I felt a pressure in my mind and images formed unbidden: a woman dressed in white sitting by a fountain; a young actress declaiming her lines on stage; a baby in a laced gown; an abbey—its bells ringing—outlined against the background of a solitary mountain; an angry mob burning a horse-drawn carriage while the horses reared, neighing in panic; the face of a woman, beautiful and pale, smiling with blood stained lips.

"Better now?"

Bécquer's voice intruded in my mind and the visions disappeared. I looked around. I was still sitting on the sofa, and Bécquer was staring down at me, his perfect features set into a mask.

"What have you done to me?"

"Nothing, really."

I checked with my tongue and found no wound inside my mouth to justify the taste of blood my mind still remembered. So the blood had not been mine.

"You gave me your blood."

He shrugged. "Only a couple of drops. Just enough to solve your problem."

"I didn't know I had a problem."

"You just told me you faint at the sight of blood. And I couldn't help but notice you were terrified of joining the party. Now, you won't be."

"Have you changed me?" I asked, my voice higher than I had intended.

"No. Of course not. You would need a lot more of my blood for that. I gave you enough to make you stronger."

"How wonderful. I don't know how to thank you."

Bécquer gave me a crooked smile. "A kiss will do."

"I was being sarcastic, Bécquer. Don't you get it? This is exactly what I was trying to explain to you before. You manipulate Federico, and everybody else, for all I know. You assume what people want and give it to them. Then get upset when they are not overjoyed by your interference."

"I meant it as a gift."

"Maybe. But even if your intentions are good, it is not all right to force your will on others. I didn't ask for this 'gift.'"

"All my lovers beg me to give them my blood. I thought you'd want it too."

"I'm not one of your lovers."

Bécquer looked away. "I'm sorry," he said after a moment. "I see what you mean. I . . . I would take it back. But I can't. The effect of my blood won't last long, though, and I promise, I will ask next time."

"You don't have to ask next time for the answer is no. I don't want your blood. I don't want to be like you. In fact, I wish—"

I wish I had never met you, I was about to say, but stopped because I didn't want to offend him. Besides it wasn't totally true. Although I'd rather not know there were immortal beings among us with powers to control humans' minds, this ancient yet childish god who had just kissed me like a lover also fascinated me. And I hoped he had learned his lesson and was not sensing my feelings, because just then, I wanted nothing better than his lips against my lips and his arms around my body. A stupid wish I knew I must stop at once.

I stood up. "I wish we would stop wasting time and join the party," I said a little too loudly.

If Bécquer was surprised at my sudden change of the conversation, he hid it well, for he just smiled and, already on his feet, offered me his arm. "Of course, my lady. Your wish is my command."

I took his arm.

Chapter Seven: The Party

Bécquer stopped by the wrought iron balustrade overlooking the ballroom and turned to me.

"Do you think you can take them?" he asked.

I looked down through the slits of the Venetian mask Bécquer had just adjusted for me. The room was big, bigger than I had thought when I spied it from the front door, and it was crowded.

Under the wheel-shaped chandelier hanging from a central beam, men dressed in suits of bygone eras and women in long evening gowns stood in small groups, gathered around the central island getting their drinks, or sat on the sofas that hugged the walls. But for the raised platform at the back of the room that supported the piano, there was no empty space on the whole floor.

My guess was that close to one hundred people were there. More than enough to send me into a frenzy any other day. But not today. For the first time ever I didn't feel like fleeing because I could sense their minds—I sensed their hopes, their uncertainties and their fears—as if I stood at the edge of their awareness. And thus, I knew that the crowd was not, as I had often imagined, an all-powerful beast ready to devour me, but made of individual human beings as flawed as I was. As I used to be. Because right then, high on Bécquer's immortal blood, I felt invincible.

I could take them, as Bécquer had put it. Even more, I was eager to meet them, to learn their stories and even discuss with them the ones I carried, still unfinished, in my mind.

An unbidden smile came to my lips. "Yes," I said.

Bécquer bent his head toward me. "So you're not mad at me anymore?" he whispered and, when I said I wasn't, he took my arm again. "Let's go, then."

We were halfway down the wide staircase when I spotted Beatriz. I recognized her by the blue shawl that barely covered her naked shoulders. She was talking to a man with a trimmed mustache and a goatee that looked too out of style to be real. As I watched her, Beatriz raised her head and her eyes met mine. I felt the ice of her stare, almost a physical touch that halted my step.

Bécquer groaned and stopped by my side. "Sorry, Carla. I was hoping to blend in unnoticed. Too late now."

As he spoke, Beatriz detached herself from the gentleman and brazenly pushed her way toward the stairs, the brouhaha of conversation ebbed in her wake, and heads turned to follow her, until everybody in the room was staring at us in expectant silence.

Basking in his guests' recognition and with the ease of a medieval king certain of his subjects' loyalty, Bécquer addressed the room.

"Dear friends, please help me welcome my new author, Carla Esteban."

He waited for the applause to subside then led me downstairs.

I felt the soothing comfort that emanated from his mind, spreading like a wave over the crowd, urging them to mingle, so that by the time we reached the floor the party had resumed in earnest. But Beatriz did not move.

"Where have you been?" she asked of Bécquer, her sharp voice belying the smile that curled her lips. "The guests were getting impatient."

"You honor me, Beatriz, to suggest anybody would notice my absence."

Ignoring Bécquer's beguiling smile, Beatriz looked up to the staircase behind us. "Where is Federico?" she asked. "He's scheduled to play in five minutes."

"Oh, yes! Federico. Right," Bécquer said lightly. "I'm afraid he won't be playing tonight."

"Really, Gustavo," Beatriz said, and by addressing him by his given name she suggested a familiarity that excluded me. "Couldn't you have waited to antagonize Federico until the party was over?"

She produced a cell phone as she spoke and started punching numbers.

In a flash, Bécquer's arm shot forward and the phone was in his hand.

"You can't ask Matt to cover for him. He's practicing now for his performance."

There was such finality in his voice that Beatriz didn't argue.

Still holding her phone out of her reach, Bécquer scanned the crowd. Soon a playful smile lit his face. "Ask Sheryl to play for us," he told Beatriz. "I'm sure she won't mind."

I followed his stare and noticed a red-haired woman holding a glass in her ringed hand while listening attentively to a middle-aged man whose crazy hair and overgrown moustache reminded me of Mark Twain.

"Sheryl is busy right now," Beatriz said. "You can't expect her to entertain your guests."

"Actually you will have her eternal gratitude if you were to interrupt her, for she would like nothing better than to get away from her present partner. She is only with him because her boss asked her to do so."

Although nothing about the perfectly made-up face of the woman betrayed her annoyance, I knew, thanks to my new awareness, that Bécquer was right.

Bécquer caught my eye as I looked back and winked at me. Beatriz was not pleased. "What is it with you, Bécquer? Why is everything a joke to you?"

"My dear Beatriz, I assure you that is far from the case, but taking the world too seriously doesn't make it a better place."

With a flourish, Bécquer handed Beatriz back her phone. "And now, if you'll excuse us. I must introduce Carla to Richard. Judging by his last e-mail, he's very much interested in her novel."

Beatriz glanced at me, her pale blue eyes cold and dismissive. I was glad for the mask that hid my features for I was certain my dislike of her was written on my face. I could read the hate on hers, as plainly as if I had sensed it in her mind. Which I hadn't. For, unlike my experience with the woman Sheryl, I couldn't read her mind. Federico hadn't either. *Why?* I wondered. Why was Beatriz different?

"I agree he's interested," Beatriz was saying to Bécquer. "It's with the subject of his interest I disagree."

"Really, Beatriz. Who is the cynic now?"

"What is her problem?" I asked Bécquer as he led me through the crowd.

She's jealous of you, Bécquer said, although he didn't really, because at the same time he was talking with one of his guests, shaking a young man's hand, bowing to a pretty woman with an ample bosom barely concealed by her low-cut dress, then moving past them, he complimented a tall gentleman on his attire, and kissed the gloved hand of his lady. So, really, he couldn't be talking to me. Yet his voice was in my head explaining Beatriz was upset with him because she had noticed he liked me.

You like me? The question formed in my mind before I could stop it. Embarrassed, I turned my head away to hide my blushing.

Bécquer laughed but didn't answer for just then we had reached the back of the room where a man in his thirties was leaning against the wall, a glass in his hand.

"Richard," Bécquer said.

The man fixed his kohl-enhanced stare on Bécquer. "Bécquer, at last," he said, his husky voice creating an intimacy that excluded everybody else. But Bécquer, his arm still on mine, nodded to him briefly and introduced me.

Limping slightly, Mr. Malick detached himself from the wall and bowed to me. *"Enchanté,"* he said.

"The pleasure is mine."

"Getting into character, are we?" Bécquer asked him.

The man smiled, drinking Bécquer in with his stare. "Not

everybody can pull Dorian Gray without make-up."

"I meant the limp," Bécquer said.

"Of course." Mr. Malick turned to me. "Lord Byron," he explained pointing at his flowing robes that consisted on the loose shirt and pants the Greek nationalists wore in the nineteenth century. "He had a congenital limp, the good lord. Mine is only temporary."

Bécquer frowned. "You mean it's real?"

"Quite so."

"You should have told me. I would have gone to see you during the week. You didn't have to stress yourself by coming here."

"Nonsense." Richard waved his hand to encompass the room. "I couldn't possibly miss your party."

"Let's get you a seat."

As Bécquer spoke, a couple sharing the sofa further along the wall got up.

A coincidence perhaps. Perhaps not, I thought as I remembered Federico's conviction that Bécquer manipulated minds.

I do not. Again Bécquer's voice was in my head as clear as if he had spoken aloud.

I glowered at him. *Stop it.*

Bécquer raised an eyebrow. *Why? It's quicker and precludes misunderstandings. Besides I like being in your mind.*

I mean it.

He shrugged and continued his conversation with Richard, a conversation he had managed to maintain even while we were engaged in our silent one.

When we reached the sofa and, after he had helped Richard to sit and asked me what I wanted to drink, Bécquer excused himself and disappeared into the crowd.

"Charming, isn't he?" Richard said, the longing so strong in his mind that it flooded mine. "You're lucky he's your agent."

"Indeed," I said, somehow insulted at the implication that it would be Bécquer's charisma and not the strength of my writing what would get me a contract.

I felt confusion in his mind, then embarrassment. "I didn't mean it that way," he rushed to apologize. "I respect Bécquer's judgment tremendously. If he has signed you, you must be seriously talented."

I laughed. His overuse of qualifiers reminded me of Madison, who couldn't leave a noun alone or use one adverb when she could use two.

"Seriously." I smiled. "I'm guessing, by your words, that, contrary to Bécquer's belief, you've not read my manuscript."

His fingers tapping nervously on his glass betrayed his embarrassment. "I may have given him that impression in my last e-mail. I promise I will read it as soon as I get home."

"Any time in the next four months would be all right," I teased him, to put him at ease, for I could sense how much he would hate Bécquer to catch his lie. "Querying is a long process. I've learned to be patient."

"A week only. And that is a promise."

"A week?" Bécquer repeated joining us.

"For my contract," I joked.

Bécquer passed me the glass of Riesling I had requested and raised his. "I'll drink to that," he said.

And we all drank.

Another of Bécquer's authors stopped by soon afterward, eager to share with Mr. Malick an idea she had just had for a horror story. She seemed surprised because she hated the genre, she explained, and all her novels so far had been realistic fiction. Bécquer encouraged her and used her presence to excuse himself and take me with him.

"You gave her the 'idea,'" I told Bécquer once we were far enough for them not to hear.

"And why would I do that?" he said, a twinkle in his eye. "To be with you?"

"Certainly not. I—"

"Actually I did," he said setting his glass—still full, I noticed—on the tray of one of the waiters passing by. "I wanted you to meet other people, and didn't want to leave him alone. Is that a crime?"

I didn't argue.

Over the following hour or so, I met many of Bécquer's authors, and several editors who requested my manuscript. Bécquer came and went freely. But whether he was there or not, the conversations flew with ease, driven by a common love of books and writing, and my enhanced ability to sense people's emotions.

It was a strange feeling being able to do so. Disturbing, yet exhilarating, for knowing how people felt, I soon realized, gave me power over them. I found it increasingly difficult, as the evening wore on, not to use it to my advantage.

Apparently, Beatriz had been successful in asking Sheryl to perform, because she had been playing for some time now. Her choices, classical piano pieces, Chopin and Beethoven mainly, blended with the discussions, never too loud to cover the voices, yet audible enough to fill awkward silences.

After each piece, all conversation ceased as a round of applause recognized her efforts, and provided an excuse, if needed, for the guests to part and regroup. I had just taken advantage of one of those breaks to take my leave from my last partner—a mystery writer I had always admired, but who, in person, had turned out to be most boring—when I spotted Bécquer.

He was helping a young woman to one of the sofas. His gesture, paternalistic and condescending as it was, was also annoyingly touching.

Bécquer looked up and his eyes met mine over the tiara the woman wore with the easy grace of a young queen. Embarrassed at being caught watching, I stumbled back and hit somebody.

A firm hand steadied me.

"Thanks," I said and turned.

Beatriz stood by my side, a glass of red wine in her hand, her eyes intent on the couple.

"Her name is Sarah," she said. "She is one of Bécquer's readers and, as far as I know, his latest lover."

"Lover?"

"Does that surprise you?"

"No. But I thought he—"

It wasn't that he had a lover what surprised me. Federico had made it clear that Bécquer had had many over the years. What surprised me was that, as Bécquer moved to take his seat by the woman's side, I had seen by the bump her Empire-style gown couldn't totally conceal that she was pregnant.

"You thought he was the perfect gentleman?" Beatriz finished for me. "Well. Sorry to disappoint you, but he has had many lovers. They don't last long, though. At the end, he always comes back to me."

I had disliked Beatriz from the moment I first met her. Just then, I plain hated her. I hated the patronizing innuendo in her voice. I hated the way she pronounced the words with the harsh edge of her foreign background that gave them the opposite meaning. And, even though I didn't want to admit it, I hated her, because she had confessed to being Bécquer's constant lover and, although I didn't care for him, or so I told myself, she seemed to think I did and she had meant to hurt me.

"Bécquer's personal life is none of my business," I said. "Why should I care whether he has a lover?"

"Why indeed?"

The sarcasm in her voice grated at my nerves. Especially because her disbelief was justifiable. Even in my ears, the harshness in my voice had belied my words.

I took a deep breath, and turned to go. Once again, my eyes fell on Bécquer and his supposed lover. She was talking and he smiled as she took his hand and set it gently on her protruding belly. I remembered then, what I'd meant to ask before Beatriz interrupted me: not whether the girl and Bécquer were lovers but whether the baby was his. For if Bécquer could have children of his own, why had he gone through the trouble of contacting and befriending Ryan?

"Is the baby his?" I blurted, my desire to know outweighing my profound dislike of Beatriz.

Beatriz laughed. "No. Of course not." There was contempt in her voice as she added. "So you don't know?"

"Know what? That he is immortal!"

Beatriz's grabbed my arm. "What else did Bécquer tell you?"

"Let me go!"

I yanked my arm, but her grip was strong and held. Beatriz pulled me closer, and as her eyes bore into mine, I felt a pressure in my mind, like a migraine about to happen. Then, as suddenly as it had come, the pressure disappeared. But her grip did not.

"You're protected." A deep frown creased her forehead. "But how . . . ?" Her eyes widened. "He gave you his blood," she finished, her voice dripping contempt. "You pathetic little human. Have you any idea of what you have started?"

Again I felt the pressure in my mind, followed this time by a stream of images, disconnected and confusing, like a movie trailer in fast forward. Images of Bécquer, his eyes glowing red, his lips curled into a snarl to reveal his canines, sharp and longer than they should be. Then as his face grew closer, unfocused, I felt the pain of his sharp teeth piercing my neck, followed by a sudden jolt of perfect bliss. By the time he pulled away, his eyes had lost their glow and were just two dark wells of sated desire. There was blood on his lips that his tongue was playfully licking.

"Beatriz!"

Shattered by the harsh intrusion of Bécquer's voice, the images disappeared, and I was back in the ballroom. But now Bécquer was before me, holding Beatriz from me.

"You liar!" Beatriz screamed.

The room had grown eerily silent, even the piano had stopped playing, and Beatriz's voice resonated hollowly against the walls. But when I looked around, expecting to find everybody staring at us, I realized time had stopped, as it had that morning in Café Vienna and the people, frozen as they were, could not hear us.

"Enough, Beatriz!" Bécquer roared. "You have no right to question me."

"You told me she was of no importance," Beatriz yelled back, seemingly impervious to the threat of his tone. "Yet you gave her your blood. When were you going to tell me I was dispensable, before or after your first feed?"

"You're mistaken. Carla is not to take your place as my blood giver."

"Isn't she? Then why? Why have you revealed yourself to her?"

"I owe you no explanation."

"I won't go easily, I warn you. I deserve to be made an immortal. You as much as promised."

Bécquer let go of Beatriz and took a step back as if distancing himself from her. "I promised nothing."

"You never denied it either. You knew it was the only reason I let you feed on me."

Bécquer laughed.

Too stunned to intervene, I had followed their conversation hoping perhaps that Bécquer would deny what I had seen in Beatriz's mind. But he hadn't. Without a trace of guilt or remorse, he had admitted it was true that he had taken her blood and had laughed at her for expecting to be made an immortal in return.

And so I had to admit that, for all his charm, Bécquer was, indeed, a monster that fed on humans, and if Beatriz was right, I was to be his next victim, his next blood giver. I turned to flee, but Bécquer grabbed my arms. Forceful, passionate, his voice broke into my mind. *I'm not a monster.*

"Get out!"

"Please, Carla. Listen to me. I never . . . "

He spoke aloud this time, but I pulled from him, screaming.

For a moment, he stared at me, his eyes not red, but black as night. Then, brusquely, he let go of my arms and, cupping my face in his hands, pressed his lips against mine, effectively silencing my crying.

As if reflected in the trembling surface of a shallow pond, an image swirled before my eyes. The strikingly beautiful face of Beatriz, a younger Beatriz, her beguiling smile and her dilated pupils that almost drowned the pale blue irises of her eyes, a teasing, irresistible call to the senses.

Beatriz, a voice whispered. Bécquer's voice, distorted in my mind.

I knew this was Bécquer's memory, a disturbing, unwanted memory. I fought it back and the image faded, only to be replaced by another, of a tearful Beatriz pleading to Bécquer to give her his blood and take her as his blood giver, followed by another of Beatriz sucking greedily on the bleeding wrist of a man's hand. The same hand I had admired this morning in Café Vienna. Bécquer's hand.

Out of nowhere a flash of pain struck me, and the images disappeared.

I opened my eyes. In front of me, Bécquer stumbled.

"Carla, go," he said. But his voice, strangled and broken, carried no power. I didn't move, but watched Beatriz step back, her eyes bright with madness, holding in her hands a broken glass red with blood.

"Bécquer!" I called and reached for him. But I was too late.

A red stain rapidly spreading on the collar of his white shirt, Bécquer fell to his knees.

Chapter Eight: Beatriz

I screamed.

I screamed and lunged at Beatriz, who was about to strike the fallen Bécquer once again. Without even looking, Beatriz pushed me aside and sent me flying against the wall.

By the time I came back to my senses and yanked from my face the crooked mask that blinded me, Bécquer and Beatriz were gone. There was shattered glass on the floor where I had last seen them and a red smear leading to a closed door.

Blood, I thought and stood, panic stricken, as I remembered Bécquer bleeding at my feet. At the sudden movement, my stomach lurched in complaint and the room started spinning. Gritting my teeth, I leaned back against the wall.

A million questions rushed through my mind. Where was Bécquer? Had Beatriz killed him and dragged him outside to dispose of his body? But that was impossible. Bécquer was immortal. Yet the pain in his mind when the glass cut his throat had been real. The glass. *Glass wounds heal slowly in immortals and the loss of blood leave us vulnerable,* Federico had told me. Beatriz knew this, I was sure, and was angry with Bécquer. Angry enough to kill him?

Bécquer and his stupid pride. If only he had told Beatriz I was his descendant, she would have understood his interest in me. But, Federico was right: Bécquer liked to play with people's feelings and was too proud to explain himself to anyone. And now he was hurt, maybe too hurt to explain. I had to find them. I had to tell Beatriz the truth about Bécquer and me. I had to stop her from harming Bécquer any further because I believed him. I believed Bécquer had not forced Beatriz to give him blood. She had agreed to it willingly. Even if Bécquer's memories were misleading, and he was in part to blame for taking Beatriz's blood, her attack on him had been unwarranted.

I took a step and the room erupted into movement and the noise exploded, deafening, in my ears, as if I had just emerged from being underwater in a crowded pool. Even the piano playing, so pleasurable before, pounded in my head. Carefully avoiding the broken glass at my feet, I made it to the door.

The corridor on the other side of the ballroom was empty.

In the diffuse light coming from the iron sconces that hung on the walls I could see several doors on the wall across, all closed, the rooms behind them in darkness. But at the end of the corridor, a rectangle of moonlight escaped through the opening of a heavily carved set of French doors.

I ran to them and slid them open. A piece of cloth lay on the floor. I picked it up. It was the blue shawl Beatriz had worn at the party. The blue shawl stained with blood.

I stepped inside and looked around, taking in the tall bookshelves, the slick wooden table and matching chairs that cast long shadows in the silvery moonlight pouring through the far wall, that was, ironically enough, made out of glass.

A noise to my left caught my attention, a moan maybe, a whisper? Then I heard his voice, Bécquer's voice inside my head, *Leave.* But it was weak, too weak to overrule my will. So instead I dashed around the bookshelf that partitioned the floor, toward the sound, then stopped. There was no need for me to go further. I had found them. I had found Bécquer, and he didn't need me, for he was lying with Beatriz in a sofa set against the wall. Bécquer, his eyes closed, his head resting on the leather armrest had his arms around her body, while Beatriz's head nested against his chest.

How could I have been so stupid to think Bécquer's life was in danger? For seeing them now, so closely entangled, I understood that, for all the drama of their exchange and her vicious attack, their whole argument had been nothing more than a lovers' quarrel. A disagreement already forgotten.

"He always comes back to me," Beatriz had told me. And so he had.

Please, Carla, leave now. Bécquer's voice was again in my mind, so weak I could have dismissed it. Except this time I had no reason to. I took a step back.

Stay!

Beatriz's call, strong and willful, stopped me. I looked up and saw her standing in front of Bécquer, blood on her bodice and a snarl on her face. "I did so hope that you would come," she said, this time aloud.

Her eyes glowed red. I froze in fear for that could only mean one thing: Beatriz was immortal.

Behind her, Bécquer struggled to get up. "Let her go," he whispered.

He reached forward and grabbed her arm. But Beatriz pulled away. "Why?" she screamed as Bécquer stumbled back and collapsed on the floor. "Why do you care so much for her?"

"He doesn't," I said.

In a flash, Beatriz was at my side. "Don't lie to me." With apparent ease, she lifted me from the ground and yanked me back against the bookshelf. "I know him. I know him better than he knows himself, and I know he cares for you."

"But it is not like that . . . He cares for me because he is . . . because I am his descendant."

Beatriz glared at me, her eyes a burning fire, and I felt the push of her mind entering mine, a harsh, painful thrust, like the prodding of a fingernail in an open wound. Then, she released me suddenly, and I hit the floor so hard my knees gave way and I fell down.

"I see you're telling the truth," Beatriz started. "I wonder why—?"

She halted, and her eyes seemed to withdraw as if they were looking inwards. One moment she was looming over me, the next she was gone, leaving behind the echo of a latch unfastening and her unfinished sentence haunting my mind.

I climbed to my feet and looked around, searching for clues of what had just happened. But for the sliding door opened to the night outside, the room was as it had been.

For a moment, I considered whether Bécquer had stopped time again and left, taking Beatriz with him. But when I looked, I saw him, lying still on the floor. I rushed to his side. His eyes closed, his chiseled features paler than ever in the soft light of the full moon, Bécquer did not answer my frantic callings. Scarier still, he had no pulse.

I panicked, at first, for no pulse meant death in my mind, until I remembered Bécquer was not human. Did immortals have a pulse?

Grateful that Bécquer's blood had made me immune to my usual blackout reaction at the sight of blood, I opened the collar of his shirt, drenched in blood, and checked his neck. A nasty cut ran from ear to ear. There was something bright inside the wound. A shard of glass.

Just as I pried it loose, two hands grabbed me by the shoulders and shoved me back.

"What have you done to him?" Federico roared. His back to me, he bent over Bécquer. Then again, he faced me. "You cut him with a broken glass and took his blood," he shouted.

For the second time that evening, his strong arms held me in the air. "I told you I would not allow anyone to hurt him."

I tried to speak but his hands were at my throat. I closed my eyes, certain I was about to die for Federico's thoughts screamed of murder. But another voice was in his mind, a tenuous presence, like a thought made out of mist, fighting his instincts.

He put me down.

"Leave," he ordered. Turning his back to me, he knelt by Bécquer.

I didn't move. "Is he going to be all right?"

Federico didn't answer.

"Beatriz cut him with a broken glass," I said. "I never hurt him."

"I know. I can sense your feelings, remember? I know your hate for him is gone."

Gently, like a mother cradles her child, Federico lifted Bécquer and set him on the sofa.

"Bécquer is my ancestor," I talked to his back, simplifying the story. "He's Ryan's ancestor too. Not his lover."

Federico looked at me. "That is why he has his picture."

I nodded.

"Is he going to be all right?" I asked again.

"Yes. But he needs blood and soon."

He needs blood. I shivered at the implications of his words. With Beatriz his blood giver gone, I was the obvious choice to replace her.

I could leave, of course, as Federico had urged me to do and for a moment I did consider leaving. But if I left, Federico would force somebody else to feed Bécquer. He had made it clear he would not let him die. I couldn't let somebody else take my place. Besides, finding this other somebody would take time, and Bécquer didn't look as if he could waste any more time. I chose to stay.

"But first we must clean his wound," Federico continued. "Any glass left inside would prevent it from healing."

I watched as Federico removed the red handkerchief from his neck and used it to clean Bécquer's cut. After retrieving several shards, he stopped and looked up.

"We need a bigger cloth to dress his wound," he explained as his eyes took in the room. "Perfect," he said, pointing beyond my head.

Faster than my eyes could follow, he left and returned holding a scarf, Beatriz's scarf I must have dropped when she attacked me. While I held Bécquer, Federico wrapped it around the wound.

"You should go, Carla," Federico told me when he finished.

"Go? But you said Bécquer needs blood."

Federico frowned, and then, as a spark of understanding lit his eyes, he shook his head. "My blood, Carla. Not yours. How could you think I would take yours?"

"I thought he needed human blood."

"No. Mine will do." Kneeling, he cut his own wrist with a knife and held the wound to Bécquer's lips.

I watched Bécquer, looking desperately for some sign of life, for although he had made Beatriz an immortal—

You're wrong. Bécquer's voice resonated inside my mind, and so relieved I was that he was still alive, I didn't fight his intrusion this time. Not even when his memories came rushing in. A fuzzy memory of Beatriz dragging a reluctant Bécquer through the library, of Beatriz drinking blood from him, of Beatriz, her eyes glowing red, staring at him with wild desire.

Good heavens, Federico yelled, moving back. *You made Beatriz immortal!*

Bécquer sat up. *I didn't. She stole my blood. Give me some credit, for Carla's sake.*

Federico stared at me. *You can hear us?*

"Yes," I said, aloud now. For only then, I realized the previous conversation had taken place inside my head.

Federico turned to Bécquer. "You gave Carla your blood?"

"What if I did?"

"Really, Bécquer. No wonder Beatriz attacked you."

"Glad to hear you approve."

"You knew Beatriz was concerned about Carla taking her place," Federico continued, ignoring Bécquer's sarcastic retort, "yet you give her your blood. What did you expect?"

"Certainly not that you'd condone her attack."

"I do not condone her action. But this wouldn't have happened if you didn't use humans."

"I don't use humans, Federico. You know quite well that Beatriz asked me to take her as my blood giver. As for Carla, you don't have to worry: she doesn't want my blood. You can ask her. When I'm gone."

Setting his hands firmly on the sofa, Bécquer stood.

Federico blocked his way. "Where are you going?"

"To find Beatriz. I must stop her before she kills someone."

"You are not serious. You cannot stop Beatriz. She's stronger than you are right now. She will kill you."

Bécquer groaned. "Thanks for your vote of confidence. But I've no choice."

"Be my guest." Bowing mockingly at him, Federico stepped aside.

I looked on, bemused by Federico's reaction, for Bécquer was shaking badly and I couldn't imagine how he was going to make it to the door, let alone confront Beatriz, this new immortal Beatriz who had lifted me with the ease of a tornado uprooting a tree.

As I feared, Bécquer didn't make it far. He took a step, then stumbled and would have fallen if Federico had not held him and helped him back to the sofa.

"I need more blood," Bécquer's voice was low, demanding. "I must reach Beatriz tonight."

"Beatriz is beyond your help, Bécquer. She stole immortality. The Elders will kill her. You know the law."

"Yes, I know the law. I sired her, thus she is my responsibility. If she kills tonight, the Elders will blame me for her digressions and kill me too."

Federico's face turned ashen. "Then I'll do it. I'll find her and kill her before she kills somebody."

"I don't want her dead. I want to stop her before it's too late."

"You can't, Bécquer. You have lost too much blood and she's driven by the unquenchable thirst of the newborn. Even if I'd give you blood, you won't be a match for her."

After a rapid nod in my direction, Federico started toward the door. But before he reached it, I heard in my mind Bécquer's voice calling his name. His silent cry, a compelling order that, even though it was not directed at me, overcame my will and sent me to my knees. Federico stopped.

Give me your blood. Again Bécquer's voice boomed inside my head, a command too strong even for Federico to resist.

Through half closed eyes, I watched him walk back to Bécquer's side, and sitting on the sofa pull down the collar of his shirt to reveal his naked throat. I looked away.

I could feel the battle raging between their minds, flashes of anger storming back and forth, hurting as if a hammer was pounding my brain.

"Enough," I shouted, not really expecting them to hear me. But immediately the voices stopped and, for a moment, only Bécquer's remained, a soothing whisper. *Block your thoughts.* Then their bickering returned.

I can't, I called to him. *I don't know how.*

Think of ice, Bécquer's voice suggested. *A wall of ice.*

I tried and failed. I tried again, until the wall remained, cold and forbidding between their minds and mine. And there was silence. A silence broken soon by the steps of someone running, getting closer and closer. Behind the sofa to my left, a door I hadn't noticed before opened and Matt stood in the doorway.

He was panting which didn't surprise me for I had heard him running, but despite his obvious hurry, he stood on the threshold, blinking, and didn't come in. The library, I realized then, was lit only by the moonlight coming through the glass wall, and for a human eye, the room would be almost in darkness. The fact that I could see clearly was, I guessed, another side effect of having taken Bécquer's blood.

While Matt waited at the door, Bécquer came to my side and helped me to my feet. "Sorry, Carla," he whispered, his fingers pushing back a stray lock of my hair. "I didn't mean to yell at you."

Before I could as much as nod, he had already reached the open door, and was inviting Matt to come inside.

Matt didn't move. "Where is Federico?" he asked, and there was fear in his voice.

Bécquer pointed at the sofa. "Right there."

"Is he hurt?"

"No. Why would you think that?"

"My mother . . . She's immortal."

"Yes. I know."

Bécquer's voice was even. But Matt's snapped. "Why? Why did you do it?"

"He didn't," Federico said, walking to them. "Your mother stole Bécquer's blood."

"You have to find her."

"I was just going—"

"To kill her," Bécquer finished Federico's sentence.

Matt stared at Federico, eyes open wide with horror. "You can't kill her. She's my mother."

"He won't," Bécquer said while Federico glowered at him. "Federico is staying here. To attend to the party," he added, shooting a warning look at his friend. Then he turned to Matt, "And I won't harm your mother. You have my word. But you must tell me where she is."

"I don't know. She came to my room and demanded I go with her. When I refused, she got furious. We were still arguing when, without warning, she turned and exited through the window. I heard the screech of tires and when I looked down, I saw her standing before Ryan's Prius. She moved as I watched, opened the driver's door and dragged Ryan from inside. I didn't see what happened next for I rushed down the stairs, but her car is gone and I couldn't find Ryan."

"She took Ryan?" I screamed and rushed to him. "Where did your mother go?"

"He doesn't know," Bécquer repeated. "But, don't worry, I can track her."

"I'm coming with you."

Gently, Bécquer grabbed my arms. "No, Carla. Your presence will provoke Beatriz, make her still more unpredictable, and hinder me. Ask Matt to drive you home and wait for me there. I'll bring Ryan back to you. I promise."

He stared at me for a moment, his mind willfully dominating mine, while his fingers traced my cheek. Then he moved back, called his thanks to Federico for giving him the blood he had stolen, and left swiftly through the glass door.

Chapter Nine: Kidnapped

When I looked back into the room, my mind aflutter with feelings I had thought long dead, Matt was confronting Federico.

"Is it true you were going to kill my mother?" he asked, his voice raw with anger and fear.

Federico didn't flinch. "Your mother stole Bécquer's blood. Among immortals, that is an unforgivable crime. Even if I don't kill her, the Elders will."

"The Elders?"

"The Elders are our rulers. They implement the law and have the ultimate saying on who is to become immortal."

As he spoke, Federico walked somewhat unsteadily to the sofa and sat down. Matt followed him. "But Bécquer promised not to kill her."

"And he won't, Matt. But if your mother kills tonight, not even Bécquer will be able to save her."

Looming over Federico, Matt screamed, "My mother is not a killer!"

"Tonight, your mother has transcended her human nature. She has instincts she has yet to master and, until she does, her thirst for blood will dominate her actions. I'm sorry, Matt; but, tonight, your mother is a killer."

Matt moaned.

Federico closed his eyes. I could feel the thirst in him, the urge to drink from Matt and his will fighting back.

Please, Carla, take Matt away, Federico's voice spoke in my mind.

And you?

I'll be all right. I just need blood.

How—?

I have some in my room.

I flinched at the image of a human held prisoner in his room. A quick smile twisted Federico's lips. *I don't drink blood from humans. I buy it in bags.*

I'll help you to your room, then.

No. I need you to take Matt away.

I grabbed Matt's arm and pulled at him. "Let's go," I said, cajoling him as I would one of Ryan's friends. "Bécquer will bring Ryan to my house. Your mother may come with them."

Matt didn't move.

"Go," Federico said. For a moment his eyes glowed red.

"What's wrong?" Matt asked.

I sensed Federico's reluctance to share with the young man his need for blood, and underneath an undercurrent of feelings quickly suppressed. I remembered how, earlier at the party, Bécquer had stopped Beatriz from calling Matt. His reasons were clear to me now. Matt couldn't come, because he was with Federico.

Yes, Federico spoke in my mind. "Nothing," he said to Matt. "I'm tired. That's all."

A light of understanding lit Matt's eyes. "Did my mother steal your blood too?"

"No. Bécquer took it," Federico said. "He needed his strength to find your mother."

"I'm sorry." Matt's voice was soft now and the anger in his eyes was gone, replaced with concern.

Federico nodded. "I'm sorry, too, about your mother."

I stepped back to give them privacy. Whatever had happened between them, it was obvious a new understanding had been reached. Federico had acknowledged Matt's feelings for him. And, judging by his present reaction, he might return them as well.

"I'll wait outside," I told Matt. After nodding my goodbye to Federico, I walked to the glass door and slid it open.

I found myself in a graveled space between the back of the house and a stone barn. Light escaped through one of the windows on the first floor, which I guessed would be Matt's room.

The white limousine Matt had driven before was parked to my right; on my left, Ryan's red Prius blocked the access to the front of the house.

The driver door was wide open, I saw when I got nearer, which evoked in my mind the image of Beatriz stepping in front of the car as it turned the corner, of Ryan braking not to run her over, and of Beatriz forcing the door open and dragging him out.

I ducked my head and looked inside the car. Ryan's guitar was on the back seat as was his blue and white duffel bag, both items sending the message no mother wants to hear: that her son is moving out. Ryan had returned home after our discussion to pack his guitar and his clothes. He was moving out, not because he was ready, but to be free of my interference. Moving where? To the couch in one of his friends' apartments? Hopefully not Emily's, for Emily, the Goth girl with whom he had been going out on and off for a year now, was still using. Or so Ryan had told me only the previous week when he'd also told me he was clean. If only I had believed him! Not that his moving out mattered at the moment. What mattered was that Bécquer reach Beatriz before she could hurt Ryan or kill him. Or make him one of them.

"Carla, my car is in the barn, would you come with me?"

Matt's voice startled me, and as I turned to face him, I saw the car key still hanging in the ignition.

"Thanks, Matt. But that won't be necessary. I'll take Ryan's car."

Matt didn't move. "May I go with you?" His reason for coming—*I want to help my mother*—hung unsaid between us.

I hesitated for a moment then nodded. "Of course." Settling in the driver's seat, I started the car.

We drove in silence at first, which suited me fine for my mind was going in a thousand directions at once covering all the possible outcomes of Beatriz's kidnapping of Ryan.

Bécquer had said he could track Beatriz. But could he? Beatriz was immortal now, and immortals, Federico had told me, could block their thoughts, hide their presence from each other. And even if Bécquer found her, what were his chances of convincing her to let Ryan go? Beatriz had been raving mad even as a human; I couldn't imagine how she would be now driven by the thirst of her newborn condition.

"I understand you hate my mother." Surprised by his words, I said nothing. Matt continued, "I hate her too, most of the time. But for all her faults, she's still my mother."

He said this matter of factly, as if there was a bond between mother and son nothing could break. I didn't argue, although in my case the duffel bag on the back seat said otherwise.

"You hate her," I repeated to keep him talking, for I didn't want to dwell on my fears.

"My mother didn't raise me," Matt said. "She left me with my dad when I was about two, while she went to pursue her career. She was a model, did you know?"

"No. I didn't." That didn't mean she wasn't famous. Unlike Madison, who studied fashion magazines with the intensity a scholar gives a rare manuscript, I had never been interested in couture.

"She was well known back then," Matt said. "Made it to the magazine covers many times. I collected them all and hid them under my bed. If my dad saw them, he never mentioned it. We never discussed her. Then, when I was about ten, he got married again, and sent me to boarding school. Mother left modeling around that time and became Bécquer's secretary. Lured by the promise of immortality, I guess. But not knowing who Bécquer was, her choice struck me as odd."

"And Bécquer? When did you meet him?"

"I saw him when Mother took me from school, at Christmas or summer vacation. He spent more time with me than she ever did. I think he liked me and I liked him too. Mother seemed to resent that fact."

"When did you learn he was immortal?"

"He told me last year when he bought his house in Bucks County. I had just finished college and was looking for a job. He offered me free room and board and a salary if I looked after the house and the grounds and drove his guests when needed. I agreed, of course. It's a great arrangement for me. It allows me to pursue my music while I build my freelance business. And the pay is good. But living so close to him, he figured I would notice . . . "

His words faded as if sucked into a vacuum that silenced the world around me and stole the air from my lungs. It was a sudden change that came and went too fast for me to understand. A second frozen in time, I would have probably dismissed as a product of my imagination, but for the image it left, burnt in my mind, of a body suspended in midair between a concrete walkway and a dark mass of water.

Come. Bécquer's voice, distorted and unreal, resonated inside my head, a command I couldn't ignore. And again a vision overtook me. This time I saw Ryan swimming, fighting the churning waters that rushed toward the opened gates of a dam.

I'll get Ryan. But you must come. Again Bécquer's voice, sounding far away yet pressing, was in my mind. Then nothing.

I swerved off the road, braking hard until the car came to a halt.

"What's wrong?"

"Didn't you feel it?"

Matt stared at me.

"Never mind," I continued, for the answer was clear in the puzzled look in his blue eyes, which I noticed were the exact shade of Beatriz's.

I returned to the road, made a U-turn, and headed northwest.

"Bécquer is at Peace Valley," I explained to Matt.

"How do you know?"

"He just told me." *Showed me* would have been more accurate for I had recognized the dam in the image Bécquer had sent me as the one closing the southwest side of Lake Galena. But I didn't feel like explaining my vision of Ryan drowning, afraid, perhaps, that saying it aloud would make it real.

"Bécquer talked to you?"

"Yes."

"You two are connected?"

I nodded.

"Is that why my mother took Ryan, to get back at you for taking her place?

Like Federico had before meeting me, Matt concluded that I was to become Bécquer's blood giver.

"No," I said, too loud to sound convincing, for the assumption irked me more than it should have. "I don't want to take your mother's position."

"But you're connected to Bécquer," he repeated.

"Yes and no. He gave me some of his blood today. The effects will wear off soon. There will be no further exchange between us. But you're right," I continued, feeling slightly guilty for screaming at him. "Your mother thought Bécquer meant to replace her."

"Mother has big plans. She wants to help people. That is why she wants to be immortal."

A part of me understood Matt's need to excuse his mother's behavior. But if the image I had seen was real, Ryan's life was in danger at this very moment because of Beatriz, and that made her my enemy. So I kept my eyes on the road, luckily empty at this late hour, for I was going well over the speed limit, and didn't answer.

We reached the lake by its southeastern shore and followed the road that surrounded the water. In the last parking lot, the closest to the dam, a car I recognized as Bécquer's BMW stood dark and alone. And empty, I confirmed after getting out of mine. Where was Beatriz's car? I wondered. Was she gone or was her car on the other side of the lake? I pushed the question from my mind. What mattered now was to find Bécquer and Ryan. I'd worry about Beatriz later.

"Let's go," I said. Without looking back to see if Matt was following, I ran toward the lake where I could see two figures emerging from the water. Two shadows in the moonlight, Bécquer and Ryan, both standing, both alive, I told myself to assuage my fears, even if one of them, the shortest one, stumbled as I watched and fell to his knees in the shallow water. The other, Ryan, stopped. Holding Bécquer by the waist, he helped him to his feet then dragged him further ashore.

Matt reached them first. He set Bécquer's right arm over his shoulders, wrapped his left around Bécquer's body, and after nodding to Ryan to indicate he could let go, started toward one of the wooden benches that dotted the lake.

I called out to Ryan, who looked up and came to me. And I took him in my arms or he took me in his. He was almost two heads taller than I was now, which made it difficult for me to hug him.

"I'm sorry, Mom."

"It's all right," I said, and meant it. Everything was all right, for he was alive.

"What happened?" I asked him as he pulled away. "Where is Beatriz?"

Ryan pointed at the upper ground that closed the lake. "She threw me in the water from up there. Why would she do that?"

"I don't know," I said, because I didn't, and because I didn't know what else to say.

"Why did she take me? Why here?" he asked, question following question as if they were just crossing his mind. "She told me Bécquer was my father. Can you believe it? She must be mad," he concluded. "For how could . . . " He frowned. "He's not." A note of concern crept into his voice as he added, "Bécquer is not my father, is he Mom?"

My guess was that Beatriz had told Ryan Bécquer was his ancestor, but now was not the moment to explain.

I shook my head. "Of course not, Ryan. I only met Bécquer last week."

Ryan sighed. "He saved my life," he said, looking over my shoulder. "I have to thank him."

Without waiting for me, he started toward the bench to our right, where Matt had taken Bécquer. I followed him.

When we reached them, I saw Bécquer sitting back, his eyes closed while Matt bent over him.

"Is he all right?" Ryan asked.

Matt's back straightened and turning to face us he pointed at Bécquer's neck. "Did my mother do this to him?" he asked me. His voice was close to panic.

"Yes. Back at the house. But, don't worry. He'll be all right," I said. I lied to calm him down, for I had no idea what was wrong with Bécquer, and the fact that his mind was closed scared me.

Matt said nothing.

"Let me see him," I said.

As Matt stepped back, I moved closer and sat by Bécquer's side.

The blue scarf Federico had wrapped around the wound was gone and the glass left an ugly, swollen wound, clearly visible. It was not bleeding now, but the collar of Bécquer's white shirt was stained with blood, as was probably his waistcoat also, although the blood was invisible against the vivid scarlet of his vest.

"Bécquer," I whispered and took his hand. It was cold like winter rain. I shivered, not only because of the cold that settled on me now with the rush of adrenaline gone and I was not wearing a coat, but out of fear that he might be dying—"We call ourselves immortals, but that name is a misnomer," Federico had told me. "We can die."

The intensity of my fear must have reached his mind, because his eyes flickered open and his voice was in my mind. *Tell them to leave.*

"He's all right," I told the two young men staring at me, "but he needs a bandage. Ryan, do you have a clean shirt in your bag?"

Ryan frowned.

"I drove your car here. Can you bring me a clean shirt?"

"Sure."

Ryan turned to go.

"Change into dry clothes, first, or you'll catch a cold," I called to his back.

"I'll do it later."

"No. Do it now. Matt can go with you and bring me the shirt."

Matt hesitated for a moment, reluctant to leave Bécquer. But Bécquer nodded at him, flinched at the pain the movement must have caused him, and whispered, "Your mother is all right, Matt. Do as Carla says."

Matt smiled, a quick smile of relief that make him look even younger. "I'll be quick," he said to me and started after Ryan.

Bécquer followed him with his eyes, and then winked at me. *I thought they'd never leave.*

Chapter Ten: Ryan

I felt relief at first upon hearing his voice. Relief that he was well enough to play games. But soon my relief gave way to anger, because I had been worried about him.

"So you were pretending," I said aloud.

"Pretending I'm half dead? No. But I wanted them gone so I can talk with you alone."

"About Beatriz?"

Your mother is all right, he had told Matt before dismissing him. Maybe Beatriz was badly hurt and Bécquer had not wanted to tell Matt.

Bécquer stalled. "Beatriz? What about her?"

"Did you ki—hurt her?"

"No. We talked. Then she left."

"You let her go?" I asked in disbelief.

"I didn't let her. She didn't ask my permission."

"You could have forced her to stay."

"Force her? Beatriz is immortal, Carla. Probably stronger than I am right now. And she had Ryan. How on earth would I do that?"

I said nothing. I could see his point. Yet I was still upset that Beatriz was free.

Bécquer bent toward me. "Why are you so difficult to please? I promised you I'd get your son back. And I did. Could you at least be thankful for that."

I blushed under his deep stare. And looked down, embarrassed at the truth I recognized in his words. "Thank you. I mean it, Bécquer. I'm grateful. Very, very grateful."

Bécquer took my hands in his. I shivered at the contact for they were still cold, even colder than I remembered. "Yet you're upset too. Why?"

"I thought you could read minds."

"Feelings. I sense feelings. No motives. No reasons. And in your case, your feelings are puzzling. So please, explain."

"Not now. You are not well," I said for his face was pale in the moonlight. "Tell me what I can do to help."

"Nothing, really. But I appreciate your asking."

"Are you sure? You seem weaker than you were when Beatriz . . . Did she do it again? Did she take your blood?"

"Yes. But this time I offered. The change demands lots of blood. She was thirsty already, so I offered her mine. Enough to carry her through the night. That will give her time to get some from one of the blood banks that deals with us immortals."

"And you trust she will."

"I hope she does. For both of our sakes. If she kills, the Elders will hold me responsible. So you see, Carla, it would have been in my best interest to keep her close so I could supervise her. But she didn't agree. She threw Ryan over the fence to make sure I didn't follow her. I had to step us out of time to keep him safe while I gave her my blood."

That explained the shock wave I felt on the road. It also explained why he had fainted. I remembered how weak he had been when I found him at the library. No wonder he was half dead now. I looked up the bank toward the parking lot. Matt was coming down already. But Ryan was not visible. He must have moved behind the car to change. He would not join us for a while. And Matt already knew Bécquer was immortal. He would not be surprised if he saw us. I turned to Bécquer.

"Take my blood," I said quickly, afraid I would lose my nerve if I thought it over. "Take as much as you need."

Bécquer smiled. "You said you didn't want to exchange blood ever again." As he spoke, he traced the veins of my right wrist with his long fingers. "What made you change your mind?"

"You saved my son's life."

His fingers stopped moving. "Is that why?" His smile was gone and his eyes were dead serious.

"Yes."

He let go of my hand. "That is not how it works. I never take blood as payment."

"But you need it."

"Matt will drive me home," Bécquer said curtly. And his words were final.

I should have felt relieved at his rejection for the idea of giving him my blood scared me more than I could acknowledge. Yet I wasn't relieved, I realized, but hurt. I pushed back the unexpected feeling for I didn't want him to sense it.

"As you wish."

I got up to leave for Matt had already joined us.

"One more thing," I heard myself saying. "I think it's better if Ryan does not visit you any longer."

"Why?" The hardness in his eyes remained, but there was a hint of hurt in his voice.

"Beatriz, of course."

"Whether Ryan is in my house or in yours doesn't matter. She knows where you live. She was my secretary, after all."

"Among other things," I wanted to say but didn't, for Matt was listening. And although he probably suspected, or knew, his mother and Bécquer had been lovers, it was not right for me to mention it now. Besides, whatever Beatriz had been was irrelevant, compared with the threat she posed now. For if she knew where I lived that meant she could hurt Ryan any time. Or Madison.

Madison. I had to call her, tell her to stay indoors, not to let Beatriz in. Or did that matter? Did immortals, like the mythical vampires of lore, need permission to enter somebody's house?

Instinctively, my hand reached for my cell, but I couldn't find it. I had left it in my purse, and my purse was at Bécquer's house.

"Madison is safe," Bécquer said.

"How did you guess I was thinking of her?"

"And Ryan will be too," Bécquer continued not bothering to answer a question that needed no answer. "I made a deal with Beatriz. If she ever touches you or your children, she is dead. Besides, she's leaving Pennsylvania tonight, she promised."

"And you believe her?"

"I do. Beatriz has risked a lot to become immortal. She won't want to antagonize me further as I am the only one who can protect her from the Elders."

"The Elders," Matt repeated. "Federico said they will kill her for stealing your blood."

"Don't worry, Matt. I'll speak in her defense. Let's hope I'm convincing." He turned to me, "As for Ryan, I'll follow your request, Carla. I won't contact him. But tell him that if he ever needs me, I will always be there for him. Or is that too much to ask of you?"

I considered retracting my request, for I could see in his dark stare the pain it had caused him to accept it and he had just saved Ryan's life. But the incongruity of the implausible events of this long day had finally caught up with me, and I felt too weary to continue the discussion. So instead, I nodded. "I'll tell him."

*

I asked Ryan to call his sister as soon as I reached the car, for despite Bécquer's words of reassurance, I needed to talk with Madison to believe she was all right. When Ryan's cell didn't work, which was not surprising after its immersion in the water, I drove us home dangerously fast along the narrow, winding road that left the lake.

The possibilities of Beatriz going after Madison were slim, I reminded myself. Besides, even if she had gone to my house looking for her after taking Bécquer's blood, Madison would not have been there. Abby's mother was supposed to pick her up at eight to drive her to her Halloween party. It was past ten now.

Madison was at the party, she had to be, and Beatriz could not reach her there.

Immortals only sense humans when they are close, Federico had told me. Beatriz did not know where the party was, or that Madison was going to a party for that matter, and she couldn't trace Madison's mind, because she had never met her.

But no amount of reasoning could convince me Madison was safe, not even hearing her voice on the phone when we finally made it home. And so, despite her complaints that I had agreed to let her sleep over at Abby's, I insisted on picking her up.

Madison was not happy to see me. And once the wave of relief at seeing she was unharmed wore off, I wasn't happy to see her either, for I soon understood why she had been so upset by my change of plans. Madison was wearing the skimpy outfit that, earlier that day, I had strictly forbidden her to wear.

I shook my head in disbelief and motioned her to the car.

"It's not what you think," Madison told me after sulking for a while.

"And what's that?"

"That I planned to wear this dress all along. I didn't, really."

"Why did you wear it then?"

"Courtney had the same cat costume I bought at the mall. She posted her picture on Facebook before the party. I couldn't wear it after that."

"Of course you couldn't."

"That's why I didn't tell you. I knew you wouldn't understand. Besides, you were not home so I couldn't ask you, could I?"

"No. But you knew I would have said no. Yet, you ignored my wishes."

"You mean I'm grounded?"

"Yes."

She thought about it for a moment. "Could we do the grounding in two weeks?"

"Because . . . "

"Isabel's birthday party is next Saturday."

"You should have thought about that before disobeying me."

"Please, Mom. I'll clean my room, I promise. And I'll keep it clean, if you let me go to Isabel's."

We argued still, but we both knew she had won. There was little I wouldn't trade for seeing the carpet of her room once again. I hadn't for ages, as it was hidden under the piles of clothes and stuff that covered her floor.

Madison disappeared into her room as soon as we got home. I wished her goodnight through the closed door, and after getting a reluctant goodnight back, checked on Ryan. He was sleeping already in the shirt he had been wearing. His jeans lay in a heap next to the bed, as they frequently had since he was a little boy. I picked them up, out of habit, and set them on the chair.

Then I took the duffel bag downstairs and emptied it into the washing machine. As I suspected, Ryan had thrown his wet clothes in with the clean ones and they were all damp now. They could have waited till morning, I suppose, but I couldn't. If I couldn't make the events of the evening disappear, I could, at least, get rid of the mud and smell of the lake from Ryan's clothes.

I sat in front of the blank TV screen while I waited for the cycle to finish, and revisited in my mind my conversation with Ryan in the car. To my relief, Ryan had not mentioned his intention of moving out and didn't argue against coming home. Even better, his version of his kidnapping did not include any supernatural twist.

Beatriz had grabbed him from his seat as he arrived at Bécquer's house, he had told me, and dragged him to her car. When he resisted she had knocked him unconscious.

By the time he came back to his senses, Beatriz was talking on her phone with Bécquer. Which was, I realized, what Bécquer had meant when he said he could track her. After a while, she hung up, turned the car around and, at neck-breaking speed, headed toward Peace Valley.

Once there, she had ordered him to get out of the car and forced him to follow her up the path to the walkway over the dam that runs along the west end of the lake. Bécquer had soon joined them, coming from the southeastern shore. There had been no exchange of words between them, Ryan told me, sounding puzzled. They had stood in silence, facing each other for a moment, and then Beatriz had lifted Ryan and thrown him over the rail. After the shock of the cold water wore off, Ryan had tried to swim ashore but the gates were open and the current pulled him toward the gap. His voice trembled as he told me how he had panicked when he realized he could not beat the pull of the water. Luckily, Bécquer had come to his aid and dragged him to the shore.

I told Ryan that Bécquer had fired Beatriz because she had stolen from him, and Beatriz had kidnapped Ryan to blackmail Bécquer out of telling the police.

I could see this explanation, as close to the truth as I could make it, didn't convince Ryan entirely, but he had not argued. Not then anyway.

I had no idea what I would tell him if, after he had time to think it over, he was to question Beatriz's or Bécquer's impossible strength, apart from suggesting he ask Bécquer and trusting that Bécquer could charm his way out of Ryan's doubts. Except that I couldn't do that for I didn't want Ryan to see Bécquer ever again, and that brought me to an impasse I had no clue how to overcome.

*

The next day started earlier as Madison missed her bus and I had to drive her to school. When I came back, I found the coat I had left at Bécquer's house hanging from the coat rack and my purse and an envelope that had not been there before sat on the table by the front door. My heart skipped a beat when I noticed Ryan's name on the envelope written in Bécquer's ornate gothic style.

Inside (yes, I looked) there was a check and a thank-you note, also handwritten. I put the envelope back and went to the kitchen where I could hear Ryan typing.

"Did Bécquer come?" I asked him, trying and failing to sound casual.

"No," Ryan said, his eyes never leaving the screen of the laptop set before his bowl of cereal. "Matt did. He brought back your things and my check for last night."

"Are you going to accept it?"

"Why not?"

"Because you didn't play." *And the check is incredibly generous*, I thought, but didn't say for I couldn't admit to having opened his correspondence.

"It wasn't my fault," Ryan said, crunching his cereal loudly. He swallowed. "Besides, Bécquer will be offended if I don't."

Something in the way he said Bécquer's name, a note of respect and trust I had heard only rarely in the voice of my students over my many years of teaching, warned me Ryan would not take well to my request to stay away from Bécquer. Yet, I had to ask.

Ryan stopped his typing and met my stare. "Stay away from Bécquer? Why should I?"

"Because . . ." Why indeed? Apart from the fact that Bécquer was immortal and could lose control and kill him without even trying, or that Beatriz had kidnapped him the previous night and could do it again, I had no reason. No reason at all to keep him from seeing Bécquer. And my real reasons I couldn't share.

"Please, Ryan. Do as I say," I finished lamely. "You don't understand but—"

"No, Mom. It's you who doesn't understand." Ryan's voice had the steel determination that over the years I had learned to recognize as the beginning of an impossible-to-win battle of wills.

"Listen to me, Ryan. You don't know Bécquer. He—"

"You're wrong, Mom. I do know him. Bécquer is cool. He

saved my life."

"Yes. I was there last night, remember?"

"I'm not talking about last night."

"What do you mean?"

"Forget it."

"Ryan. If you don't tell me, I'll ask him."

"Oh, so it's all right for you to talk to Bécquer, but not for me?"

"Don't change the subject. What do you mean when you say he saved your life?"

"It's no big deal. I OD'ed once, and he took me to the hospital."

I dropped on a chair by his side, for my knees felt like rubber and I would have fallen otherwise. "You were using drugs in his house?" I asked in a voice so high-pitched I barely recognized it.

"No. Of course not. He wasn't with me when I used. I was hanging out with friends."

"Where?"

"What does it matter where? It was a party. I don't know how it happened. I don't remember much. I was high. We all were, I guess. The next thing I remember I was at the ER. And the doctor said I had OD'ed. And Bécquer was there. He was the one who took me to the hospital. He asked me not to tell you."

"Great. And since when do you do what strangers ask?"

"Bécquer is not a stranger."

"No, of course not. You have known him for how long? Five seconds?"

"He took me to NA meetings," Ryan said, ignoring my sarcasm. "I thought you'd appreciate that."

"He took you to . . . Why did you never tell me?"

"You never asked."

I stopped arguing. I knew when I was beaten. Which was about every time I had had an argument with him since he turned five.

I got up and poured myself a cup of coffee. Caffeine was the last thing I needed at the moment, but I was not thinking straight.

What other things was I not aware of that Bécquer had done for my son? Was Ryan moving in with him the previous night? Had Bécquer agreed to that, or was Ryan crashing with Matt? Probably, I would never know. I returned his duffel bag to his closet while he was sleeping and put his clothes back in the drawers. My guess was he had not noticed.

"Don't worry," Ryan said when I returned to the table. "I have so much homework, I won't have time to practice with the band, so I won't be seeing Bécquer for a while in any case."

"You never told me you were in a band."

"I did tell you. Shut up and listen."

"Excuse me?"

Ryan looked up and frowned. "What did I do wrong now?"

"You just told me to shut up."

"No, I didn't. Shut Up and Listen is the name of the band."

We sat in silence. The clicking of the keyboard the only sound punctuating my contradictory thoughts. After a while the sound stopped. Snapping his laptop shut, Ryan got up.

"I've to go. My first class starts in half an hour."

I nodded.

Ryan bent over and kissed the top of my head. "It's okay, Mom. Don't worry. I still love you."

"It's good to know, baby, for I love you too."

"I know," he said.

And after hugging me with his free arm, he rushed to the door.

Chapter Eleven: Bécquer's Request

I tried to write after Ryan left but couldn't. The bizarre events of the last twenty-four hours continued to play in my mind—as they had through the long sleepless night I had endured—blocking my creativity. At times elated, at times overwhelmed by the memories, I found it impossible to concentrate on my writing. So, eventually I gave up and went for a ride.

That I ended up in the parking lot overlooking the dam in Lake Galena was not planned, yet it seemed inevitable. Two other cars were there when I arrived. But not Bécquer's. My disappointment at Bécquer's not surprising absence was all too real to ignore. Yet absurd.

I locked my car and went down the bank to the gravel strip by the water where Ryan and Bécquer had come ashore.

A heron, white and slender, walked the shore hunting for food. The heron I had described in the manuscript Bécquer had agreed to represent. Was it only the previous morning I had signed my contract with him?

But for the heron, the place was deserted. The boats and canoes that dotted the lake in summer were grounded ashore on the crescent-shaped inlet to my left. And the owners of the cars sitting by mine were nowhere in sight.

Turning my back to the lake, I walked to the bench Bécquer and I had shared the previous night and sat down.

The weather had been unusually mild this past October and the trees had just reached their full autumn colors, but the stunning beauty of my surroundings failed to impress me.

Maybe it was because the effect of Bécquer's blood had worn off during the night, and after perceiving the world through immortal senses, it seemed dull now that I was seeing it with my human eyes. Maybe it was, plain and simply, because Bécquer was not with me and I wished he were.

Which, again, was absurd.

I barely knew Bécquer. I had met him only on three occasions and always at a professional level. Bécquer was my agent. Only as such had he invited me to his party. Yet, the intensity of his stare when he ordered me to drink his blood, back in his room was filled with the passion of a lover. Or was my memory deceiving me matching my own desires?

I got up abruptly and dashed up the path that led to the dam. The gates were closed now and, unlike the whirlwind of emotions fighting in my mind, the water was still. Neither down at ground level, nor up where I stood on the walkway, did I see any sign of Ryan's brush with death, nor of Bécquer's confrontation with Beatriz. As far as the world was concerned, it could all have been a dream.

But it had not been.

Ryan had almost died there the previous night, and I, after knowing Bécquer for less than a day, had become obsessed with him. How stupid could I be? Bécquer was a 200-year-old man who drank human blood and manipulated people' wills. Yet, hard as I tried, I couldn't keep his dark stare from my mind or his deep, beguiling voice from haunting my thoughts. And his smile kept coming back, threatening to destroy the barriers I had so carefully erected around my heart.

I had lost my heart once long ago when in my twenties. The irrational thinking that ensued had carried me into a marriage, followed by years of self-loathing, a direct result of my husband's unrelenting mental abuse, and resulted in a bitter divorce.

I would not lose my heart again.

At least this time I knew I was not the only one to blame for my weakness. My infatuation with Bécquer was too sudden and intense to be real, which meant that, despite Federico's reassurances to the contrary, Bécquer had charmed me. The solution to this unwanted situation was, thus obvious: I had to break all connections with him.

And the safety of my heart was not the only reason for doing so, for the more I dwelt on the events of the previous night, the more I realized that accepting Bécquer as my agent had been an invitation to disaster. What had happened with Beatriz had not been an isolated incident, an accident that would not be repeated, but a warning of worse things to come. A reminder that if you play with fire, you're bound to be burned, or, in my case, that accepting Bécquer's help to get my book published could get my children hurt.

And that was a price I was not willing to pay.

Bécquer, for all his charm and impeccable manners, lived on human blood. How could I ever justify this? And if I didn't, I couldn't justify using his non-humans abilities to my advantage, either. Federico had admitted Bécquer used his charm to push his authors. The look of adoration in Richard's eyes the previous night at the party left me no doubt he was already half sold on buying my book. His reasons had nothing to do with the quality of my writing or the strength of my story, for he had not read my manuscript yet.

Yes, I believed my book was good and deserved to be published, but was I ready to compromise the safety of my children or my peace of mind for this to happen?

The answer was no. Absolutely no.

I had to call Bécquer and tell him I didn't want him to be my agent, and hope he would agree to rescind our agreement on the basis that he had not played fair with me. The real me, the rational me, would have never signed, yet the previous day, I had done so, willingly, after a slight, almost nonexistent hesitation. This could only mean Bécquer had influenced my decision, and if he had, the contract was not valid.

But the logic of my reasoning was lost on Bécquer.

"I did not force you," he told me, and, even though the phone

I could sense the outrage in his voice at my suggestion. "You knew I was immortal when you signed."

"I didn't know you were drinking Beatriz's blood. I didn't know you fed on humans."

"No, you didn't," he admitted. Then, after a pause, "Would you come over to discuss this further?"

So you can use your charm to change my mind? "I'd rather not."

"Federico is here," Bécquer insisted. "You can talk with him, as you seem to trust him while you don't trust me."

"No, Bécquer. I don't think so."

"What if we meet in a neutral place? Café Vienna tomorrow at ten o'clock?"

"Are you crazy?" Federico's angry voice came through the receiver muted, then stronger as he addressed me directly, "Carla, would you mind waiting a couple of days to make your decision?"

I heard Bécquer swearing in the background, just before the line went dead.

I set the phone down, confused. I had practiced my conversation with Bécquer a thousand times while driving home. None of my imaginary exchanges had ended like this. Why had Federico interrupted Bécquer? Why did he want me to wait?

Before I could find an explanation for their strange behavior or gather the courage to call again to clarify my position, the phone rang, startling me.

"My deepest apologies," Bécquer said after I picked it up. "Federico thought we were engaged for the next few days. He was mistaken. In fact we can meet tomorrow. Please say yes. I promise I won't influence you, and, if after our conversation you still want to break our contract, I will abide by your decision."

I said yes, of course. How could I not when he put it that way? Only to realize after I hung up that if I had so easily agreed to his request on the phone, my chance to deny him anything in person was close to nil.

*

I was early the next day for my meeting with Bécquer. It had been a conscious decision. Being first, I thought, would give me an advantage, or at least, save me the embarrassment of walking the length of the room under his stare.

The place was almost empty when I arrived—too late for the morning rush, too early for lunch—and in no time I was sitting at one of the tables by the window, my espresso forgotten in front of me, watching the door. As I waited, I questioned the wisdom of my decision for every time the door opened my heart jumped in my chest and the mantra I had chosen to repeat to keep me calm lost a little of its effect.

Somewhere outside the chimes of the town hall clock sounded the hour. Any moment now, I thought, but I was wrong. Bécquer was not the next person to come in, nor the following one. By ten thirty, my mantra had changed from "*I'm in control*" to "*He's not coming*," and my nerves stretched to the point of breaking.

I was considering leaving when the door opened, once again, and Federico appeared in the doorway. Federico, and not Bécquer, my mind registered, whether with disappointment or relief I was not sure.

My first thought was that Bécquer had sent Federico to drive me to his house and, bracing myself to resist such a request, I waited for him to come over. But Federico stalled by the door. Holding it open with his body, he was maneuvering a wheelchair through, when one of the baristas, a girl with ginger hair, as natural looking as Madison's bleached blonde, rushed to his aid.

I imagined the man in the wheelchair to be an acquaintance of hers, for despite the long line that had formed by now to order, the girl didn't return to her post behind the counter, but stayed by the door talking to him.

Across the room, Federico's eyes met mine. He shrugged, and I nodded and looked away, embarrassed he had caught me watching. Out of the window, the cars coming down Main had stopped before the light. And again, like Sunday morning, a blue convertible was first in line. The roof was down, and I couldn't see the driver, but the car I was certain was Bécquer's.

"Sorry, I'm late."

My heart stopped at the sound of his voice, Bécquer's voice, inside the cafe, addressing me, while his car stood outside. I turned, startled, and met his eyes staring at me. His eyes, dark and serious, at a level with mine, because Bécquer was sitting. Sitting in the wheelchair Federico had pushed through the door.

Bécquer in a wheelchair?

"Bécquer," I whispered, my voice entangled with too much feeling. "What happened?"

Bécquer shrugged, or tried to, for his neck was encased in a collar brace that limited his movements. "I fell down the stairs," he said, a wink in his eyes belying his words.

His face, his handsome face, was criss-crossed with pale scars. And as I looked down to hide my shock at his condition, I noticed he held his right arm in a sling against his chest, and the right leg of his dark suit had been cut lengthwise to accommodate the cast.

"My apologies, Carla," Federico said moving from behind Bécquer. "To get a wheelchair took us longer than anticipated."

"And it was totally unnecessary," Bécquer said. "I could have walked."

"You could not," Federico said, a note of frustration in his voice.

Are you crazy? Federico had asked Bécquer on the phone the previous day when he offered to meet with me. Now I understood why.

"I would have waited," I told Federico, "had I known."

Bécquer scowled. "No. You wouldn't. You wouldn't have believed me had I told you. In fact, you still don't believe me, and you are looking at me."

He was right. While my eyes had taken in the details of Bécquer's condition, my mind refused to admit it, for Bécquer was immortal and immortals heal immediately. Were Bécquer's disabilities real or was he pretending to be disabled to manipulate me?

Bécquer swore, making no secret that he had read my thoughts.

"Do you really think so poorly of me?"

He tried to stand as he spoke, but managed only to hit the cast against the floor before Federico stopped him. "If you don't sit still, I'll take you home."

Bécquer moaned. "It's not my fault. She doesn't believe me."

"Give her time," Federico said, in Spanish now and somehow I knew he had checked to be certain nobody in the café could understand our mother tongue, before he added, "After all, for someone who is supposed to be all powerful, you are quite a sight."

"Thank you for reminding me," Bécquer answered in the same language. "Are you trying to cheer me up or push me to despair?"

"Neither. Just let Carla adjust, then ask her what we discussed at home and, please, be quick. Immortal or not, you should be lying down, not driving around."

They stared at each other for a moment in silence and I knew they were talking mind to mind. But, to my regret, I could not hear them. I didn't need any immortal's powers, though, to feel Bécquer's simmering anger and frustration with his condition. In the end, it was Bécquer who looked away, and Federico's tight grip on the armrest of the chair eased.

With a sigh of relief, Federico turned to me. "Your espresso has grown cold," he said unexpectedly. "And I blame myself for it. May I get you another one?"

I looked down at the cup, still full, in front of me, and shook my head. "It's all right. I like it cold."

Bécquer raised an eyebrow in mock disbelief, and I felt myself blushing at being caught in a lie.

Federico smiled. "Please, oblige me." With a last, warning look at Bécquer, he went to join the line.

I followed him with my eyes, reluctant to face Bécquer just yet, this sulking, wounded Bécquer whose sorry state had already broken my defenses. How was I to deny him anything in his condition?

I shouldn't have come, I thought for the thousandth time.

"Carla?"

Too late now. I turned to face him.

"Do you still want to terminate our contract?"

I nodded, not really listening, for my mind was still struggling to make sense of Bécquer's situation. "How? I mean, who did this to you?"

Bécquer only stared.

"Beatriz," I whispered.

It was the only explanation. But Bécquer denied it. "Beatriz is gone, Carla. You don't have to worry. She won't harm your children. And I assure you my present disability will not interfere with my role as your agent."

"That's not why I asked."

"Out of pity then? Please don't. I'm immortal remember? I will heal before the week is over. And, in the meantime, would you reconsider your position and give me a chance at being your agent?"

He raised his left hand as if to stop me from answering, while he continued, "I've already queried several of the editors as a follow-up to our conversations at the party. If I were to withdraw your manuscript now, it would be unprofessional on my part and awkward for you or another agent to resubmit to them. So before you decide to rescind our contract, please realize that doing so would harm my credibility and yours.

"As for your fears, I assure you they are unfounded. Beatriz is gone and I already gave you my word that I won't talk with Ryan without your permission."

"I'm afraid my permission is redundant. Ryan is eighteen and has a mind of his own. He has refused to stop seeing you. *And I don't even know if I have the right to keep him from you.* "You saved his life. Twice," I said aloud. "And took him to NA meetings. Why didn't you tell me?"

"I should have told you," Bécquer said and sounded contrite. "In fact, I should have asked your permission. I apologize for overstepping my boundaries. You are his mother. And I am no one to him."

"That is not true. Ryan thinks highly of you."

"He does?" For the first time, a smile touched his lips. But even then there was pain in his eyes. "Thank you for telling me."

"You're welcome."

"So, going back to the contract," he continued after a moment. "Would you meet me half way? Would you agree to let me represent you until we get an answer from these editors? If one of them wants to buy your manuscript, I'll represent you just this time. If nobody buys it, then you are free to contact other agents. Does this seem fair to you?"

Fair? Fair had nothing to do with my desire to part with him. But of my two reasons, the first one, my fear of Beatriz's retaliation, he had refuted, and the second, my attraction to him, I couldn't mention. I couldn't even think about it, for if I did he would sense it in my mind and could use it to charm me even more. And "more" was the key word, for obviously his charm was working already.

I nodded. "All right."

Bécquer beamed at me. "Great. I will tell Matt to type a contract with the new clause and fax it to you."

"Matt is your secretary now?"

"And my driver."

That explained my seeing Bécquer's car at the light before. Matt must have dropped Federico and Bécquer then went to find a parking space. As for Matt being his secretary, did that mean he was giving him blood too?

"No," Bécquer answered my thoughts. "Matt is not my blood giver. Funny that you'd think that when it was that same assumption on Federico's part what brought me to my present state."

"Matt did this to you?" Shocked at his words, I forgot to complain about his intrusion in my mind.

"No. Not Matt. Federico."

"Federico?"

"That's what I said."

"But how? Why?"

"He found me drinking from Matt."

I flinched, for if I had read the signs correctly Federico had more than a passing interest in Matt.

Bécquer nodded when I suggested it. "If I didn't know then, my broken bones would have convinced me by now."

"Why did you drink from Matt?"

"He offered."

"You could have said no."

"No. I couldn't." And as I looked at him unconvinced, he added, "I was unconscious."

"Matt offered me his blood at Lake Galena," Bécquer explained at my insistence, "and I said no. Then he helped me to his car and drove me back home. The guests were gone and the house empty when we arrived, Matt told me later for, by then, I had already passed out. Matt went in to get me some bags with blood from Federico's room. When he didn't find any, he panicked for he thought I was dying and decided to cut his wrists and give me his own.

"I drank from him, by instinct I guess, from his wrists first, then from his neck. When I came back to my senses Federico was looming over me shouting, and Matt lay unconscious in my arms.

"Before I had time to understand what was happening or make sense of it, Federico dragged me out of the car. I tried to explain but he wouldn't listen. Instead, he hit me. My senses still dulled by my recent loss of blood, he caught me unaware and the force of his blow sent me flying against the library wall. My neck snapped when I hit one of the metal beams and severed my spine. Then the glass broke and fell on me."

"Your face—"

"My face, my arms, my body. I have more cuts than I can count, and broke more bones than I thought I had. Not to mention the fact that I was paralyzed from the neck down."

"But your arms, your legs, you can move them now."

"Sure. But it took me all night to regenerate my spine."

I winced.

"Nothing to worry about, really, Carla. My bones are set now. The collar brace, the sling, the cast in my leg, they are just a precaution."

"Federico seems to disagree."

"Because he feels guilty and likes to keep me like this to order me about."

"Federico loves you, Bécquer. He's trying to help you."

"He loved me, you mean. He loves Matt now. I'm no more than an inconvenience for him."

"I don't agree. Federico may not be in love with you anymore. But he still cares for you."

"Why are you defending him, Carla? Federico is responsible for this." He waved his hand as he spoke to cover his brace, his arm, and his leg. "You know, he overreacts when in the throes of passion. You were with him when he broke the steering wheel of my car. Yet you seem to think I'm the one to blame."

"Sorry, Bécquer. I'm really sorry that you got hurt."

"You're sorry?"

"Yes, of course."

"Then, maybe there's still hope for me."

"Hope?"

"I was not totally forthcoming before when I said I'm all right. My bones may have mended already, but the cuts from the glass will take longer to heal for some were deep and traces of glass may still remain in others."

He took my hand. A move I had not anticipated, and at his touch, a shiver ran down my spine. An unlikely reaction for his hand was warm.

"Federico swears the blood he buys in bags is all he needs,"

Bécquer was saying. "But even he recognized human blood would help me heal faster and agreed to drive me here today so I could ask you."

"Ask me—?"

"Whether you'd be my blood giver."

Chapter Twelve: Rachel

I stared at Bécquer in total shock, appalled at his asking me to be his blood-giver.

"I guess not," he said when I didn't answer. His eyes staring straight into mine were not pleading.

He let go of my hand and leaned back in his chair. He looked tired, exhausted even, the dark circles under his eyes ever so visible on his fair skin that was crisscrossed with pale scars.

"Does it hurt?" I asked him.

"Not at all." A spark in his eyes, again he bent forward, and then winced—a sign of pain that negated his enthusiastic denial. But Bécquer, as if oblivious to his own discomfort, continued eagerly, "The interchange is quite pleasurable, in fact. And it doesn't have to be for long. A week perhaps. I will not ask you to stay after I'm whole again, I promise. I will give some of mine in exchange. Taking immortal blood will make you stronger. It will also extend your life and—"

"That is not what I meant."

Bécquer frowned. Then, the shadow of a smile playing on his lips, he added, "So will you do it?"

Yes, my body screamed, with yearning for the power his blood had given me the previous evening.

"No," my reason answered. "I told you I didn't want to share blood with you."

"Yes. You told me that before the party. But later you offered it to me."

"And you refused."

"And I would not be here begging, if I had accepted it. So, you see, we all make mistakes. I'm no hero, Carla. I want this to be over. But I'm no demon either. I have no devious plan for you afterward."

The strangest thing of all was that I believed him. I believed he didn't mean to force me to stay when he didn't need me any longer. I believed him. It was me I didn't trust.

I had tasted his blood only once and was already finding it almost impossible to resist its lure. How could I trust myself to give up drinking it after I had taken it for a week? And if I stayed longer as his giver, wouldn't I end up like Beatriz, wanting its powers so badly I would steal it to become immortal?

"You are not like Beatriz," Bécquer said. He was using his powers to sense my feelings so he could convince me to do his bidding. If I could, wouldn't I use them too? To anticipate my children's mistakes? To keep them safe? To be there when they got in trouble, like Bécquer had done the day he took Ryan to the ER?

"Beatriz had her agenda, her grandiloquent expectations of saving the world. You wouldn't steal my blood."

"You don't know that."

"I have had many blood givers. None of the others turned rogue."

Could it be because you manipulated their minds like you are manipulating mine? I thought but didn't say aloud because I was too busy fighting the urge to agree.

I pushed my chair back.

Every breath hurting as if the air had frozen inside me, I got up. "I'm sorry, Bécquer, but I can't."

I saw pain in his eyes, a flash of anger, before his features settled into a mask, a beautiful mask of cold disdain. "As you wish."

Before I could answer, Federico's deep voice came from behind. "Took forever but here I am."

He came forward and set a tray with three cups on the table, three espressos black and steaming, while shooting a warning look at Bécquer. When he finished, he turned to me, "Carla, you're not leaving now, are you?"

I nodded, for I didn't trust my voice would not break were I to speak.

"But you can't. You mustn't," Federico said, blocking my way.

I felt the undercurrent of a silent conversation going on between them and the sense of loss at not being able to hear their minds hurt almost like a physical wound. I had to go, I knew, or I would agree if only to stop that yearning.

"I'll be leaving soon," Federico continued. "And this may well be the last time we see each other. I would hate our acquaintance to end like this, in a hurried goodbye. Would you please humor me and take a seat?"

I found myself obeying his soothing voice. For a moment, I wondered whether he was using his charm on me, but rejected the idea. I genuinely liked Federico and wanted to talk with him. Besides, who in her right mind would say no to a chance to be with him?

Federico smiled and, after I moved aside my cold espresso, he handed me a new one.

"Where is my latte?" Bécquer asked, his sharp words covering my thanks.

Unperturbed by Bécquer's demanding tone, Federico placed one of the cups in front of him. "You didn't tell me you wanted a latte."

"No, I didn't. You're right. I didn't because you didn't bother to ask."

Federico sat down. "Gustavo, you don't drink. So, really what does it matter which kind of coffee I brought you?"

Bécquer glared at him. "And that shows how much you know me. I don't need to drink. That doesn't mean I don't enjoy drinking coffee. And when I do drink it, I like it with milk. So, I'd really appreciate it if you'd get me a latte. I'd go myself, except you have made it very difficult for me to do anything on my own just now."

Federico's eyes glowed red for a moment. Then, he turned and glanced at the counter where the line almost reached the door. When he looked back, his eyes were back to normal. "I'm sorry. But it would take me too long. Would you be so kind as to drink your coffee black just this time?"

"Fine." Reaching forward, he lifted his cup.

Bécquer was right handed, I knew, and, his right arm being in a sling, he was using his left hand. Still, it seemed to me, he was inordinately inept with his left one. Or maybe he was weaker than his relaxed attitude had suggested for his hand was trembling, his movement so shaky, I had to stop myself from leaning forward to help him.

But if Bécquer needed help, I reasoned, Federico would have offered it. Federico shrugged when I looked at him, and, grabbing his cup abruptly, drank his coffee in one gulp.

The coffee had been too hot for me to take more than one sip, but Federico didn't show any sign of distress. Unlike Bécquer who, as the rim of the cup touched his lips, winced. In Bécquer's hand the cup trembled, the steaming liquid spilling over his fingers. Bécquer swore as the cup slipped from his grip and hit the table, coffee splashing in all directions.

Federico stood and wheeled Bécquer chair back. "Really, Bécquer. Was that necessary?"

Bécquer said nothing, but stared toward the counter while Federico offered him a white handkerchief he had produced from the pocket of his jacket to dry his hand.

I got up to fetch some napkins from the island by the door. When I came back, the girl with the ginger hair who had greeted Bécquer before was by his side. The nametag on her black top read Rachel.

I set the napkins on the table and sat down. The napkins were unnecessary for Rachel had already wiped the table with a cloth. She was fussing over Bécquer now, while Bécquer stared at her, at her cleavage more precisely, for the girl was leaning over him. Visibly upset, she gushed excuses and apologies as if she were the one to blame.

"Are you sure you didn't burn yourself?" she asked.

Bécquer shook his head and smiled at her, with that maddening smile of his that could melt ice.

"Let me see." She took his left hand in hers. "Oh no!" she said as she examined his fingers. "You did burn yourself. I'll bring you some ice."

"That won't be necessary, Rachel." He pronounced her name slowly, rolling the R so that he was almost purring. "It is just a small burn. In my circumstances," he waved his hand slowly to include his broken leg, his arm held in a sling, and the collar brace around his neck, "it does not signify."

The girl let out a nervous giggle. "May I at least bring you another coffee? Latte, isn't it?"

Bécquer beamed at her. "That would be lovely."

I followed Rachel with my eyes, frustrated at how much Bécquer's flirting with her bothered me. Without making a conscious decision, I stood again.

"I have to go," I said to no one in particular and, grabbing my coat from the windowsill, I started for the door.

This time, Federico did not try to stop me, but when I got to the parking lot he was waiting by my car.

"Other door," he said, pointing at the front of the building. "I didn't mean to startle you. I came to apologize for Bécquer's behavior and beg you to reconsider his proposal of becoming his blood giver."

"Did Bécquer send you?"

"No. He's too proud or too stupid to do so. Probably both. But he's hurting and he needs you, so I came in his stead."

"You're wrong. He doesn't need me. Not anymore. He has found a new giver."

Federico sighed. "Yes, I guess Rachel would do anything for him at this point.

"But don't let his shameless flirting mislead you. I don't think Bécquer cares for the girl. He's probably charming her to cover his hurt at your rejection."

"Are you saying he's using her? And you are all right with that?"

"Don't be so harsh on him, Carla. Bécquer was eleven the first time he tasted immortal blood. And although he remained human for many years, I think a part of him stopped growing that day. When he's upset, he reverts to being that child."

"To be hurt is not an excuse to hurt others. If he behaves like a child, you should treat him like one. Don't defend him, Federico. Let him make his own mistakes so he learns from them. Maybe then, he will finally grow up."

"You're right, Carla. He needs to grow up. That's why he needs you." As if pre-empting my denial he hurried on, "Yes, I know Rachel would gladly give him her blood. But Bécquer needs someone like you who loves him for who he is, not a girl worshiping a god who doesn't exist. Would you agree to come, if he promises not to charm her?"

Too tired to deny his assumption that it was because I loved Bécquer that I didn't want to be around him, I shook my head.

"No. Even if he doesn't charm this girl, there will be others. And I'm not you, Federico. I won't accept that."

Federico nodded. "I understand," he said. "Your decision is wise and I'll abide by it. Loving Bécquer was for me an agony I do not wish on anyone."

"Take my card," he added, offering me a card he had somehow magicked into his hand, "in case you ever need me."

"Goodbye, Carla," he continued after I took it. "I hope you find a new love soon. For only another love displaces—even if it does not erase—the previous one."

I thanked him for I knew he meant well, even if another love was the last thing I wanted. As for forgetting Bécquer I was certain that, in my case, absence would do as well.

Chapter Thirteen: Gustavo Adolfo Bécquer

I dreamed of Bécquer that night. Dreams of wanting and desire that only increased my determination to stay away from him. If my subconscious was sending a hint, it wasn't a very subtle one. But my waking self would have none of this nonsense. Determined to forget him, I forced myself to sit and started typing at the computer.

Not for long. The characters usually so eager to tell me their story were nothing but flat cutouts that morning, and the flow of words soon died on my fingertips.

I gave up after a while and googled Bécquer's name: Bécquer, Gustavo Adolfo. I had studied his work at school back in Spain, and still knew some of his poems by heart, but if I had learned anything about his life, I had forgotten since. In my search, I found two or three pictures of him in old style suits, but neither these photographs, nor the romantic portrait his brother Valeriano had painted of him (the one printed on the Spanish currency of the twentieth century), bore but a faint resemblance to the man haunting my dreams. As for the biographies I found online, they were sketchy to say the least. They provided the bare facts, but no insight into his mind:

Bécquer was born in Sevilla in 1836 and lost his father when he was six. At eleven, after his mother's death, he and his six brothers went to live with one of their mother's sisters and several years later, he moved alone with his godmother.

Later he would reunite with one of them, Valeriano, when at fourteen, he joined his uncle Joaquin's studio as an apprentice. Like their father, like their uncle, Valeriano chose painting as his profession. Bécquer, although talented as a painter, loved books more and dreamed of becoming a writer.

His dreams, and almost nothing else, he took with him when, at seventeen, he moved to Madrid with two of his friends. He survived, barely, by writing for newspapers and magazines, and coauthoring plays while working the odd clerical job he was ill-suited to maintain. At twenty-one, he fell sick with the first bout of the mysterious illness (TB was suspected) that would eventually kill him at thirty-four.

With the care of his friends and of his brother Valeriano, who by then had moved to Madrid, he recovered. After a chance encounter, he fell desperately in love with Julia Espín, a beautiful actress who would become his muse even after she rejected him and married another.

After another bout of illness, he married Casta Esteban, his physician's daughter. A marriage, unexpected that, as Bécquer had told me, ended in separation.

I read on, devouring any information I found about him. And so I learned that Bécquer died in 1870—stopped being human, that is. Before dying, he asked his friends to burn his letters, and publish his poems and stories because he was certain, he told them, he would be better known after his death than he had been in life. A presumption that turned out to be true. A presumption he could well make come true if, as an immortal, he supervised the success of his published work.

After a while all the information I found repeated these bare facts. I stopped reading and ordered all the biographies I could find about Bécquer, including one written by one of his friends and another by Julia, Valeriano's daughter, named after Julia Espin, the beautiful girl who broke Bécquer's heart and inspired his achingly beautiful poems of unrequited love.

I wrote nothing that first morning, which bothered me. My first book, a medieval fantasy—not surprising, considering I taught Medieval History at a private college—had taken me two years to write. When I finished my second book two years after that and realized that the end was not an ending but the beginning of a new story, I'd decided to take a sabbatical to finish my third book, for I was beyond tired of writing in stolen moments. My sabbatical had started in July; we were in November now. I had no time to waste.

What was even more frustrating was that, although my dream of getting successfully published was within my reach now that Bécquer was my agent, knowing he was immortal had stolen all pleasure from my accomplishment. Not to mention the fact that my infatuation with him was making it impossible for me to concentrate on my writing.

Still, I persevered. But after two days of wasting time rereading Bécquer's *Rhymes and Legends*, or daydreaming in front of an empty screen, I gave up on writing my novel. Instead, I started an account of my encounter with Bécquer and the impossible events that followed.

I was aware that publishers take months to read a manuscript, yet knowing Bécquer's powers of persuasion, I was not surprised when a week after our meeting in Café Vienna, he contacted me by e-mail.

Two of the editors who had read my novel were interested, he explained. One of them was, as I'd expected, Richard Malick, the editor impersonating Lord Byron I had met at Bécquer's party. Bécquer attached the two proposals and discussed the pros and cons of the two offers and the reasons he recommended I sign with Richard.

Finding no fault with his decision, I wrote him back agreeing to his suggestion.

His next e-mail was short and to the point.

Dear Carla,
Richard will be at my house this Saturday for the purpose of signing your book contract. Would you kindly join us here at 3 p.m.?
As we discussed, this will terminate my representation of your work.
Sincerely yours,
Gustavo Adolfo Bécquer

Although it was my understanding that most contracts are signed by mail, his tone, courteous and professional, gave me no reason to refuse his request. But my trust of his word was not the only reason I accepted. The truth was I wanted to see him.

His hold on me had increased, not decreased, as the week passed. Several times, I found myself driving toward his house while running an errand, or after dropping Madison at school or at one of her friend's house. I had always stopped in time and turned around. I couldn't start to imagine my embarrassment had I made it close enough for Bécquer to sense me and my pathetic crush. For crush was the only word to describe this yearning for a person I had met only four times. And having a crush at my age was ridiculous. Crushes were for teenagers, not for mothers of teens.

Madison might be only fifteen, but she, certainly, had more sense than I did.

"I don't fall for guys who have no interest in me," she had told me some weeks earlier. "What would be the point?"

"There is no point," I'd told her. "But you don't choose whom you love."

"I do," Madison said, so stubbornly certain that I gave up trying to explain.

But I knew by experience that reason had nothing to do with love. I had fallen for Bécquer against all common sense and, hard as I tried, had not been able to forget him. And against my better judgment, I wanted very much to see him again.

Besides, the meeting was to be the following Saturday, which was the weekend Madison would be grounded. And any excuse to leave the house was welcome, because nobody knows better than a grounded teenager how to make life miserable for everybody else.

Chapter Fourteen: The Contract

There were two cars already in the parking space in front of Bécquer's house when I arrived. A yellow Jeep and a green Honda Civic.

Almost two weeks had passed since the Halloween party, which meant Federico would be gone by now and Matt, I knew, kept his car in the garage. My understanding was that only Richard would be there today. I remembered Richard had mentioned he didn't own a car for he didn't need one in Manhattan and had taken the train to Princeton to come to the party. Maybe he had rented one today. If he had, a Jeep seemed an unusual choice for a rental. Was his the Honda Civic then?

As for the other, it had to be Rachel's, I thought with a pang of jealousy that had no reason to be there. Bécquer had asked me to be his blood giver and I had refused. That he had chosen somebody else was inevitable, that I hurt because he had was illogical.

My hurt also validated my decision. Even if I had agreed to give him my blood, he might have taken the girl as his lover, which would have been even more painful for me. I had done the right thing. By staying away from him I would eventually forget him. I just needed more time. I would have plenty of time from then on, considering I didn't plan to see him again.

Yet this thought that was supposed to reassure me only added to my distress.

How had this happened? Since when had my desire to see Bécquer overcome my wish to sell my manuscript? Today my dream would come true. I was about to sign a two-book deal with one of the most prestigious publishing houses in the country. I should be elated, but I was not. I was upset and apparently jealous because a young, pretty girl had caught Bécquer's attention.

I tore my eyes from the small sedan blurred by the raindrops streaming down my window and, forcing myself to bury this futile yearning for a man who was not human and thus forbidden, I turned off the ignition and stepped outside.

Behind the curtain of rain that fell unrelenting from an overcast sky, Bécquer's house loomed in front of me, its impressive mixture of modern architecture and Pennsylvanian charm more apparent now without the orange lights that had framed it on Halloween night.

Holding my umbrella with both hands to fight the gusts of wind that threatened to yank it away, I dashed across the gravel expanse, and climbed the stairs to the porch. The door opened before I knocked and a young woman appeared in the opening. Although her face was in shadows, my suspicions were confirmed when I recognized Rachel, the red-haired girl from Café Vienna.

"Come in," Rachel said, moving brusquely aside. "Bécquer is waiting."

It sounded like a reproach the way she said it, as if she was accusing me of making him wait. But I wasn't late, I knew, and as if to prove me right, the antique clock sitting in the hall sounded the hour.

Without glancing back, the girl disappeared into the great room. She obviously meant for me to follow but I hesitated as I considered the puddle forming in the wooden floor underneath my umbrella.

"Excuse me," I called to her. "Could you tell me where to leave this?"

The girl stopped and turned and for the first time she met my eyes. She was young. Younger than I remembered. Ryan's age was my guess. Or maybe she seemed younger because, unlike at Café Vienna, she was wearing no make-up. And in her pale, freckled face her eyes showed red. Not flashing red that would have marked her as immortal, but red and swollen, as an indication that she had been crying. In fact, she seemed about to burst into tears at any moment as if my question had pushed her over her limit.

"It's all right," I hurried on, "I'll leave my umbrella outside."

I grabbed the doorknob but, before I could turn it, a young

man materialized by my side.

"Please give it to me," he said. His deep baritone voice was surprisingly gentle as he addressed the girl. "Don't worry, Rachel. I'll take care of this."

He was young, mid-twenties probably, with broad shoulders and muscled forearms his tight sweater couldn't conceal and, unlike Rachel who seemed overwhelmed by emotion, his manners were brisk and efficient.

After he relieved me of my coat and umbrella, he offered his hand. "I'm David," he said.

"Carla Esteban."

David smiled. "Rachel will take you to Bécquer's office," he told me. "And Rachel?" he called as the girl waited for me to join her, "try to smile."

If anything, Rachel seemed even more distressed by the young man's attempt to lighten her mood. Tears welled in her eyes.

Had Bécquer tired of her already? But that didn't seem right. If he had, Bécquer would have stopped charming her and she would have forgotten him. Bécquer was not cruel that way, or so Federico had led me to believe.

Not knowing what else to do, I offered the girl a tissue. She thanked me and, after drying her eyes, slid it into the pocket of her jeans and started again across the great room with the grand piano at one end, and through the door that led to the corridor where I had followed Beatriz after she injured Bécquer the night of the party. But instead of turning toward the library, Rachel stopped before the door directly across and knocked.

"Come in," Bécquer called from inside. Bécquer's beguiling voice invited me in. I felt like fleeing, but it was too late. It had been too late for a long time. Probably since the moment he had told me he liked my book the first time I ever met him.

In my struggle to keep my feelings at bay, I almost missed the quiver in the girl's voice when she announced my arrival.

"Thank you, Rachel," Bécquer said. "You may leave now. But please come back in half an hour for I will need you to make some copies."

Rachel nodded, and then turned and left.

From behind the massive mahogany desk where he sat, Bécquer stared at me.

"Please come in," he said and smiled. The smile lit his handsome face, which was paler than I remembered it and somehow thinner. But his eyes, dark on mine, did not smile.

I mumbled my welcome, and stepped forward toward the empty chair that Bécquer indicated with his hand. Before I reached it, I sensed a movement to my left and turned just in time to see Richard stand.

"You remember Richard?" Bécquer asked.

"Of course."

I had been so intent on keeping my feelings blocked from Bécquer's mind, I'd failed to notice the man who held my future in his hands. But Richard seemed undaunted by my omission, if anything he seemed nervous, for his voice was louder than necessary, his smile brighter than meeting me, an almost unknown author, would warrant.

"We just finished discussing the last points of your contract," Bécquer said to me after we were all seated. "Do you want me to read it to you now?"

I shook my head. "Actually I'd rather read it on my own."

Bécquer started.

"Sorry, I don't mean to insult you in any way. But I find it difficult to follow when someone reads aloud." *Especially if it's you,* I thought but didn't say.

"I understand."

He didn't carry his arm in a sling anymore, but as he handed me the document over his desk, I noticed several scars on his hand just before his fingers touched mine. I shivered.

"You can move closer to the fire," Bécquer said, "if you are cold."

I noticed then there were, indeed, some logs burning in the fireplace, which surprised me for I had assumed immortals didn't feel hot or cold. Maybe I was wrong. Or maybe Bécquer had lit it for us.

I shook my head. "I'm fine," I said, although I wasn't. But it wasn't the fire I wanted to get closer to. And I wasn't cold either.

The contract was typed this time and simply written. It covered all the points I wanted covered and some I had not thought about. I handed it back to him when I was finished and thanked him for his hard work for the contract was clearly in my favor.

"Shall we proceed then?" There was a hint of relief in his voice.

As I nodded, he produced a black fountain pen and signed first, above his printed name. Then Richard got up and, coming to the table, added his signature below.

"I hope our partnership continues," Richard said handing me the pen, "after these two books are done and sold. And I hope—"

What he hoped for I never knew, because just then, Bécquer reached forward to take the contract I had already signed, and as he did his pen rolled out of his reach. Richard jumped forward and grabbed it as it fell. His eyes on Bécquer, he set it on the table. Bécquer glowered at him.

Before any of them spoke, there was a knock at the door. Following Bécquer's invitation, Rachel came in and, taking the contract from the table, moved to the copying machine by the farther wall.

Soon she was done and, after handing a copy to each of us in a black folder, she left as silently as she had come.

Richard looked at his watch. "I better go," he said, getting up, "if I want to catch the five-thirty train."

He bent over the desk as he spoke and shook Bécquer's hand—with both of his—for a long time and with an eagerness that betrayed his deep affection for him and made their previous silent confrontation even more puzzling.

"I'll call you tomorrow," Richard said.

Bécquer nodded, his face unreadable, but when Richard asked

me if I could give him a ride to the train station and I said yes, Bécquer's eyes, once more, flared with anger.

"That won't be necessary," he told Richard. "Rachel will take you, as agreed."

"I really don't mind," I said. Both because I had time to do so and because it was obvious to me that Rachel was too upset to drive. She had not uttered a word while she was in the room, and her hands had shaken when handing us the copies.

"But I do," Bécquer said. And as I looked at him, nonplussed, he added, "I need you to stay a moment longer so we may discuss the termination of our contract."

"Another time, then," Richard said brightly, shaking my hand. He had turned his back to Bécquer so Bécquer couldn't see his face, and, as he spoke, his eyes sent me a message I failed to understand. I frowned; Richard sighed in frustration, and turning toward Bécquer, repeated his goodbyes.

"Please, sit," Bécquer told me as the door closed behind Richard.

"My job as your agent is done," Bécquer continued after I complied. "I sold your manuscript. Our contract is now finished, and so according to your wishes I have prepared a termination clause to end our partnership. Just take your time to read it and let me know what you think."

I swallowed hard and took the paper he offered. The clause was short and simple and took only two minutes to read. I looked up.

"Is everything as you expected it?" Bécquer's eyes held mine, challenging me to argue. A challenge I didn't take for there was nothing to argue.

"Yes," I said, my mouth so dry that saying that single word hurt.

He handed me a golden pen. "Would you sign then?"

I didn't move. Bécquer was right. It had been my wish to terminate the contract. And the reasons for my request were still as valid now as they had been a week past. Being around immortals will always pose a threat to my children. Yet, if I signed Bécquer would disappear from my life as though he had never existed. And I was not ready for that.

"Carla!"

I blinked and averted my eyes for I realized I had been staring at him.

"I've already signed," he added.

Forcing myself to move, I took his pen and signed my name beside his.

"Great," Bécquer said. Then he smiled sheepishly. "Would it be too much to ask that you make a copy for your records? Rachel is not here at the moment and I'm afraid modern technology eludes me."

"My pleasure," I said, trying hard not to roll my eyes in disbelief. I was by no means a technological genius, but being unable to make a copy sounded lame even by my standards.

"I took the liberty of contacting Sarah," Bécquer said while I set the paper on the glass and pressed start.

"Sarah?"

"Sarah Lindberg," Bécquer said. "She interned with me some years back. She runs her own agency, now. You may have met her at the party."

I grabbed the original and the copy still warm from the printing and walked back to his desk.

"She was quite pregnant," Bécquer continued, and when I nodded, he continued, "I thought she would be a good match for you and she agreed. If you want, I'll give you her phone number so you may contact her at your convenience."

Once more, I was having trouble concentrating under his stare and, again, I failed to answer.

Bécquer frowned. "Unless you have another agent already, of course."

"Of course," I repeated, then, realizing how little sense I was making, I quickly added. "No, I don't. And thank you for talking to Ms. Lindberg on my behalf."

Bécquer nodded. "Sarah will be on maternity leave for several months starting soon. If that is a problem I could suggest somebody else."

I smiled. The idea I could finish another book in a couple of months was quite laughable considering I was still struggling with the sequel I had just agreed to produce for Richard, because my outline kept changing between the happy ending I had planned when I started and a darker apocalyptic one that fit my somber mood of late. As for the hypothetical novel Ms. Lindberg would be representing, I had not even started it.

"No, that won't be necessary. I can wait."

I grabbed my purse, readying myself to leave, but Bécquer didn't move.

"One more thing," he added, motioning me to sit again. "I would appreciate if you don't mention to Sarah the real reasons for our parting."

"Of course. I couldn't possibly tell her that—"

"That you mistrust me?"

I flinched at his directness. "Well, yes. No, I mean, what did you tell her?"

"The official story. That I'm retiring."

"But it's not true."

"Actually, it is."

"But you weren't, were you, when you signed me?"

"Things have changed since."

"Because of Beatriz?"

"Among other reasons."

"Sorry."

"Don't be. I have been an agent for over ten years. Ten great years. Good things are not meant to last forever."

"What will you do now?"

"Something exciting, I'm sure," he said lightly. But his eyes avoided mine.

I waited for him; he hesitated as if he were about to add something. But just then, the phone rang.

Bécquer looked at the number on the caller ID and scowled. "Would you mind?"

He grabbed the phone when I said no, and after the required greeting was over, put the caller on hold. "I apologize but I do have to take this. David will walk you to the door."

As if on cue, there was a knock and David came in.

"It has been a pleasure working with you, Carla."

His handshake was firm, his voice professional, and the mind behind his guarded stare already miles away.

"Likewise," I said and meant it. For meeting him had been a pleasure, before the events that followed turned my life into a nightmare. And now our parting would put an end to the nightmare and things would return to normal. But, although I was perfectly aware that I was the one who had rejected him as my agent, the one who had refused to give him my blood, I didn't want to leave. Only his casual dismissal, his unconcealed eagerness to return to his call stopped me from asking him to forget everything I had ever told him and begging him to take me back.

Instead, I tore my eyes from his perfect features, lit now by a smile that was not meant for me, and followed David to the hall.

Somehow I managed to stay still while I waited for David to bring me my coat and my umbrella. I even managed to thank him, and not to trip as I climbed down the stairs. and walked back to my car.

The Honda Civic was gone. Which meant it was Rachel's car, I thought as I ran to mine, the rain pounding on my head because I had not bothered to open my umbrella. After unlocking the car door, I threw my purse and umbrella on the back seat and climbed inside. Finally safe from unwanted stares, I leaned back against my seat and let the sense of loss wash over me.

It was done. I had severed my connection with the immortals. My children were safe, and my life back to where it had been before meeting Bécquer.

Except it wasn't. For I had met him and fallen for him. And, for all my reassurances that I would soon forget him, leaving still hurt.

A sharp knock startled me. But when I blinked my eyes open, the only sound I heard was that of the water hitting my windshield.

I reached forward to start the car. Again, I heard the sound, a persistent tap coming from my right. And as I turned toward the sound, I saw a face framed in the window. Richard's face.

I was so surprised to see him there that I just stared. Then, before I could hit the button to lower the window, Richard opened the door and slid into the passenger's seat.

"I hope you don't mind my intruding," he said, while my eyes took in his smart trench coat glistening with rain. "But you did say you could drive me to the station. Does your offer still stand?"

I nodded. "Of course."

"Good." He shot a nervous look over his shoulder. "Then let's get out of here before Bécquer sees us together and calls me back."

Chapter Fifteen: Richard

"I was waiting for you in David's car," Richard explained as I put the car in reverse.

"Why? Why didn't you leave with Rachel?"

"Because I wanted to talk to you." His voice sounded tense, and a quick glance at him as I looked over my shoulder to make sure it was safe to back up my car, was met with a cold stare from his pale blue eyes.

My stomach sank with apprehension. Was Richard thinking of breaking his contract with me now that Bécquer didn't represent me anymore? Despite my previous realization that my interest in Bécquer overruled my desire to get published, the thought hurt more that I cared to admit.

"About our contract?" I asked, glad that the sound of gravel cracking under the tires and the constant pelting of the rain had drowned the quiver in my voice.

Richard snorted. "The contract? Is that all you care about?"

Too shocked by the suppressed anger boiling in his questions, I said nothing.

"Could you at least pretend you care for Bécquer a little after all he has done for you?"

I stopped the car at the end of the driveway, and turned to him. "Would you please explain what this is about? You're obviously upset with me and I've no idea why."

Richard stared at me for a long time. Finally, he ran his fingers through his blonde curls that, wet with rain fell flat over his forehead, and shook his head. "You really don't know?"

"Know what?" I was angry now because something in his expression had scared me, and anger seemed a better option than to follow up in that fear.

"I see you don't," Richard said. "Could you please drive on? I'll tell you what I know, I promise. But I've already missed the five-thirty train and I'd like to get home before nine. I have to walk my dogs."

I hesitated for a moment then nodded my agreement. After taking a deep breath to release the tension building in my muscles, I turned on to the road and headed toward Princeton.

"First, I want to apologize for my harsh words," Richard started, his voice loud enough to be heard over the grating sound of the windshield wipers. "I assumed Bécquer had shared the news with you, and I was appalled by your lack of concern."

"News? The only news Bécquer ever shared with me was in regard to my book. Bécquer is my agent, Richard. He does not discuss his personal life with me."

"You mean, he never told you about his car accident on Halloween night? He did say he had been the only one hurt, but because you two left the party together, I thought you had been involved in the crash."

A car accident on Halloween night? So that had been Bécquer's official story. So that was why Richard was worried, because Bécquer had been hurt? He was right to be concerned, for his wounds had been serious, fatal even, had he been human. But Bécquer was immortal, and thus Richard's concern, unwarranted.

Relieved that a simple misunderstanding was behind Richard's fears, I loosened my grip on the wheel, and answered him lightly. "No, I wasn't with him."

"You don't seem surprised, though."

"I wasn't with him when the accident happened. But I did know about it."

"You knew?" Anger crawled back into his voice. "You knew and you don't care? You knew and yet, today, you come to the meeting and act as if nothing has happened and never even ask him how he's doing?"

"I—" I started, then stopped, confused. Why was Richard mad

at me? Bécquer had told me he was almost healed when we talked the previous Tuesday. And today he had looked perfectly all right.

But when I told Richard this, he was not appeased.

"Bécquer is not all right, Carla. He will never walk again."

It took a moment for his words to sink in, then, when their meaning finally hit me, my mind went blank. My body reacted instinctively and my foot pushed hard on the brakes. The tires skidded on the wet road, causing the car to swerve in and out of the right lane.

Richard yelled and reached for the wheel. I pushed him hard, rejecting his help, rejecting his words. But his scream had broken the standstill in my mind and my brain was once again in charge of my body, and soon I had the car under control. Somehow I steered it into the shoulder and brought it to a halt.

For a moment we just sat there, side by side, the sound of the rain not covering, but underscoring, the silence that had fallen between us.

"What was that about?" Richard said at last, sounding more dazed than scared. "You could have gotten us killed."

"I'm sorry. But, really, it was your fault. Why did you say that to me? Why did you make up such a horrible lie?"

Richard's look of shock melted into something else, something like pity, which scared me even further. "So, Bécquer didn't tell you."

"No, of course not. Bécquer didn't tell me because it is not true. You just made it up now to . . . to . . . " But for all I wracked my brain to think of a reason I came up empty.

"I'm afraid I didn't make it up, Carla. And, again, I apologize for misjudging you. Had I known you do care for him, I would have broken the news to you more gently."

I braced myself against the wheel. "It's too late to spare my feelings now. So please, just finish your story."

"Do you want me to drive?"

"Drive?" I repeated, then, as I realized we were still on the shoulder when we were supposed to be driving to catch a train, I put the car in gear. But my movements were shaky, my vision blurred. I shifted again into park and nodded to him. "If you don't mind."

"Bécquer did not give me all the details," Richard said after we'd exchanged seats. "All I know is that he was doing better after the accident. Then this past Monday, Rachel found him unconscious in his study. She called 9-1-1 when he didn't respond to her attempts to revive him, and they rushed him to the hospital. Later that night, he came back to his senses. Apart from not remembering what had happened to bring him to that point, his mind suffered no damage, but his spine had been irreversibly broken. There is no doubt on his prognosis. He will never regain the use of his legs."

I said nothing for I could not find my voice.

Bécquer is immortal. He's not paralyzed, a part of my mind repeated, convinced perhaps that if I said it enough times it would be so. But another part of me was remembering my recent meeting with Bécquer, and, as it did, details I had ignored came to the foreground as if forced from my subconscious by Richard's words.

Bécquer had been sitting when I came into the study and never got up during the meeting, not even to say goodbye. Conveniently, when I was ready to leave, somebody had called and prevented him from accompanying me.

As for his bizarre claim that he didn't know how to make a copy, it made perfect sense now. It had been an excuse to avoid getting up. Bécquer was almost 200 years old. He had grown up in a world without technology, but he had learned how to drive, and knew how to use a computer for he had sent me e-mails. How could I have ever believed he was too stupid to know how to work a copy machine?

So, yes, it was possible that Bécquer was paralyzed and had tried to hide it from me. But that didn't mean his condition was permanent. In fact, it couldn't be, for Bécquer was immortal.

Then another detail came to my mind. His reaction when his pen rolled out of his reach had been slow. And losing it had been clumsy to start with. Bécquer, the immortal Bécquer I remembered from the party, from our meetings in Café Vienna would not have dropped it. I started to shake.

Richard released a hand from the wheel and touched my arm. "Carla. Are you all right?"

I started at his touch, but didn't push his hand away. "Yes," I lied and closed my eyes, overwhelmed by a sense of loss so intense I felt like drowning. Bécquer, the perfect immortal who had so impressed me, was gone, replaced by an injured man forever dependent on others.

No. My mind fought back. Bécquer could not be mortal and paralyzed. Federico would have told me. Federico knew I loved Bécquer. Why had he not contacted me?

According to Richard's account, only Rachel had been with Bécquer at the time, which meant Federico had left before Bécquer was fully recovered. Did he even know about the accident?

"Who is Federico?" was Richard's answer when I asked him. "Is he Bécquer's friend?"

"Yes. They have been friends for many years. Just friends," I hurried to add to quench the note of hope I had noticed in his voice. "If you don't mind, I'm going to call him now."

I was aware I couldn't talk freely to Federico with Richard sitting next to me. But I needed Federico's reassurance that Bécquer would be fine.

I reached back for my purse without waiting for Richard's answer and grabbed the phone and Federico's card. But when I punched his number on my cell, my call went directly to voice mail.

"Will this Federico come to stay with Bécquer?" Richard asked after I finished recording my message.

"I hope so."

"Good," Richard said, sounding relieved. "And until he does, would you agree to check on him?"

"You want me to check on Bécquer?"

"Yes. Actually it was because I wanted to ask you this that I waited for you. I don't think it's good for Bécquer to be alone right now."

"But he's not. Matt lives over the garage. And—"

Richard shook his head. "Not anymore. Rachel told me Matt left last week."

"What about Rachel?"

"Rachel doesn't live with Bécquer."

"They may not live together but they—" I stopped, embarrassed when I noticed the trace of jealousy trailing in my voice.

Richard took his eyes from the road and shot a glance in my direction. "Lovers. Is that what you think? That Bécquer and Rachel are lovers?"

I nodded.

"You're wrong. They are not lovers. I'm sure of it."

I disagreed. Even if I had not seen them flirting in Café Vienna, Rachel's behavior today was proof enough that her feelings for Bécquer went well beyond a simple boss-secretary relationship.

"If, as you say, they are not lovers, why was Rachel so upset today?"

"I didn't say she didn't care for him. The distress she showed today obviously suggests she does. But Bécquer does not care for her that way, or he would not have fired her. Today was her last day with him."

I thought about it for a moment. I wasn't convinced. "It may be her last day as his secretary. That does not mean she won't continue seeing him."

"Yes, it does. Rachel told me Bécquer was adamant. He strictly forbade her to come back any more, which means Bécquer will be on his own. I don't think that's a good idea."

"But he can't be alone. Doesn't he need help?"

"Yes, of course he needs help. That's why he hired David and two other nurses who take shifts around the clock. I was talking about friends."

"I don't think Bécquer thinks of me as a friend. He didn't even tell me he was incapacitated."

"Maybe he didn't tell you because he cared too much and didn't want your pity."

"He cares for you, Carla," Richard told me when I said nothing. "I saw the way he looked at you at the party. I would have given my soul for him to look at me that way. And I was not the only one to notice. Beatriz was jealous of you, so jealous that she quit that very night. What more proof do you want, Carla?"

He had gotten it all wrong, but I couldn't tell him the truth. I couldn't tell him Bécquer only cared for me because I was the descendant of his wife's third son. I couldn't tell him Beatriz had left because she had stolen Bécquer's blood and become immortal. And I was too ashamed to tell him that, regardless of the fact that Bécquer didn't love me, I was in love with him.

"I don't know what happened between you two that night that makes you doubt him so. But I know he still cares for you. He has never pushed me so hard to read a manuscript in the ten years I've known him."

"That might have been because he wants to finish all his projects before retiring."

"Retiring? Did he tell you he was retiring?"

"But he mustn't," he added frantically after I told him what Bécquer had said. "He shouldn't make such a big decision right now. Bécquer loves being an agent and he's good at it. Of course he's upset now, but he won't always feel that way. His clients would understand if he takes some time off. Losing the use of his legs and his career at the same time could be too much, even for someone as strong as he is."

"Are you suggesting he may be thinking of killing himself?"

Richard remained silent for a moment as if considering my question. Then he shook his head. "No. Bécquer loves life too much for that. But he needs help to adapt to his new situation. He needs friends. Knowing he has decided to retire only makes my request more pressing.

"Please, Carla, promise me that you'll check on him tomorrow and on the following days, as often as he will allow you to visit him. I don't want him to be alone."

I promised. Not only because he was right that Bécquer should not be alone, but also because I wanted to know the truth. Was it true that Bécquer was human? And if he was, who had changed him and why? The only explanation I could think of was that the Elders had punished him for making Beatriz immortal. But if they had, where was Federico? And why hadn't he told me?

Chapter Sixteen: The Consequence

After I dropped Richard at the station I called Madison to let her know I was coming home. The call was mainly for my own peace of mind, because, as usual, she didn't seem to care whether I was in Princeton or being eaten by a shark, as long as I was back in time to chauffer her around. And right then, as she was grounded, she had no need for me.

I had just crossed the toll bridge over the Delaware and was back in Pennsylvania when my phone rang.

"Carla? Can you talk?" Federico's voice broke through the speaker, his Spanish accent thicker than I remembered it.

"Bécquer is not answering his phone," he continued, after I confirmed I was alone.

"Have you tried his cell?"

"Yes," he said. Switching to Spanish, he rushed on, "Both his house and his cell. Have you seen him? Are you sure he can't walk?"

I pulled to the shoulder because I didn't trust myself to drive, and told him about our meeting, Bécquer's confession that he was retiring, and Richard's account of Bécquer's accident and of his staying at the hospital.

"Hospital?" Federico interrupted me. "Bécquer was at the hospital?"

"He was unconscious when they found him. Rachel called an ambulance."

"Don't you see, Carla, if he is still immortal—"

"—they would have noticed he's not human."

"Exactly."

"But he is immortal, isn't he? He is still immortal."

"I don't know, Carla. Something is wrong."

"You mean it's possible for an immortal to become human again?"

"*Sí,*" Federico said after a slight hesitation. "*Es posible.* The Elders have the power to do so, and Bécquer did break the law by making Beatriz immortal, but even if they made him human, he shouldn't be paralyzed. He was walking when I left him."

"You knew the Elders could make him human and you left him alone? How could you? Why didn't you wait until the Elders had passed their sentence?"

"I never thought they would apply such penalty given that it was Beatriz who stole his blood. Besides, why do you act so surprised that I left? You know I'm only allowed to be with Bécquer for a week and you were the one who told me I had to let him make his own mistakes, if I wanted him to stop acting like a child."

Yes. I had said that. Maybe the fact that my children never followed my advice had pushed me to giving it too freely. If people were going to listen to me, I would have to be more careful, or more precise, when expressing my opinions.

"I didn't mean it literally, Federico. I didn't expect you to leave him when he was still in recovery."

"He was doing much better when I left," Federico insisted, "and he had Rachel to care for him. Obviously it wasn't enough and now he's in trouble. So, at the risk of eliciting his fury, I'm coming to check on him."

"Do you want me to pick you up at the airport?"

"No. Matt will drive."

So that's why Matt was not with Bécquer anymore. I should have guessed they were together, for their mutual attraction had been evident last time I saw them, but somehow, the thought had not occurred to me.

"Matt—" I stopped. Whether Matt and Federico were together was none of my business. "Where are you now, Federico?"

"Washington. Washington, D.C., which means we'll be there later tonight, but until we arrive, could you please go back to Bécquer's house, and stay with him?"

"I . . . I don't think it's a good idea. Bécquer chose not to tell me of his condition. I think he will hate to see me now."

"I don't care whether Bécquer hates it or not. I just don't want him to be alone tonight."

"David, his nurse, is with him," I argued because I found the idea of intruding into Bécquer's private life so late in the evening intimidating.

"A nurse? A nurse he could trick without even trying. You don't know Bécquer as I do, Carla. It's not like him to push a publisher to sign a book contract in such a hurry. That, and the fact that he's retiring, troubles me."

Federico sounded relieved when I told him I would stop at Bécquer's on my way home. "I'll take care of everything when I get there, I promise. But could you please contact me after you see him? Or better still, tell Bécquer to call me?"

I called Madison again after my talk with Federico, to let her know I might not come home until much later. When she didn't pick up, I sent her a text message.

It was close to seven when I drove up the narrow driveway and into the expanse before the main entrance where I had parked in the afternoon. The Jeep was still there, which meant David was in the house. Or so I hoped, because, apart from the two lamps flanking the front door, the house stood in total darkness.

I turned off the engine and stepped outside. The bang of the door closing, the cracking of the gravel under my feet, the beep from my car lock, the snap of the doors locking, each and every sound came back eerily amplified against the black silence that surrounded me.

Somewhere along the way, the rain had stopped but the clouds still must have covered the sky, for I could not see a single star and the house loomed in front of me, an imposing shadow against the dark sky.

I hesitated as I reached the stairs. It was clear visitors were not expected at this time, or welcomed, and at the thought of facing Bécquer or, worse still, of having him refuse to see me, filled me with such dread, my whole body hurt with the urge to flee. But my promise to Federico bound me to at least try.

Forcing my legs to move, I climbed the steps to the porch and knocked. Nobody answered. I knocked again, slamming the iron knocker hard, then grabbed the knob and twisted it. To my surprise, it turned under my hand and the door opened.

I stood still, for a moment, straining my eyes to see. It was even darker inside, the only light being the one coming from the porch. No, not the only one, for, after a moment, I saw a faint glow to my right. Then, I heard a sound, the unexpected sound of someone cheering.

"Bécquer?" I called. When there was no answer, I crossed the hall into the great room, and then stopped.

The glow, I could see now, belonged to a game playing on a TV screen. On the sofa facing the screen, someone was sitting.

"Bécquer," I repeated, louder this time. When he didn't move, I turned the lights on to get his attention.

As the iron chandelier above us came to life, the person on the sofa jumped to his feet.

He's standing, I thought. Bécquer is standing. Relief washed over me —relief and embarrassment. If Bécquer was all right, I had no reason to be there. But when he turned and I saw his face, I realized my relief had been premature, for it was David, not Bécquer who was looking at me. David holding the video game controller in his hand as if it were a weapon to fend off an intruder.

"Ms. Esteban?" Recognition replaced the surprise on his face. "What are you doing here?"

"You didn't answer the door."

"What?" he asked, loud enough to be heard a mile away.

I touched my ears and David dropped the remote in the sofa and jerked his headphones off. He smiled apologetically, "Sorry."

Disappointment and anger fought in my mind because David's presence reminded me that Bécquer was disabled and in need of help, help David could hardly provide if he was so intensely engaged in playing a game. "Aren't you supposed to be attending to Mr. Bécquer?"

David raised his head defiantly at the accusation implied by my words. "Mr. Bécquer has already retired for the night."

I glowered at him in disbelief. "That is no excuse. What if he needs you?"

"He would call me on my cell," David said, producing a phone from his pocket.

"That's not good enough. Bécquer's not answering his phone. Maybe he dropped it and can't reach it."

"Or maybe he's just sleeping."

"Let's hope that is the case. You didn't hear me knocking or coming in, and, according to Federico, you didn't answer the house phone either. A most irresponsible behavior. So, if you don't want me to report you to your employer, I'd appreciate it if you checked on Mr. Bécquer right away and ask him if he would see me."

"Now? But he's probably sleeping."

"It's only eight o'clock. Isn't it a little early?"

"He was tired after the meeting," David said, his tone clearly stating this was none of my business. "He went directly to his room and asked me not to disturb him. He even canceled his dinner."

Dinner? The image of Bécquer having dinner resonated strangely in my mind. Bécquer was an immortal and immortals do not eat. Not human food, anyway.

"Did he eat the other days?" I asked, before realizing how stupid I sounded.

David looked at me, nonplussed. "Yes, of course."

Of course. I shivered with apprehension. Could Federico be right? Had the Elders changed Bécquer back to being human? The signs that this was true were becoming more difficult to ignore. And yet, I didn't want to believe it because if Bécquer was, indeed, human, his retiring struck me as being as bad an omen as Richard had made it sound.

"I need to talk to Bécquer," I insisted. "Either you go and ask him whether he'll see me, or I'll go to his room."

I turned toward the stairs when David didn't move. His voice stopped me. "Mr. Bécquer is not in his old room. It was not practical for him to live on the second floor."

Too late, I realized that knowing where Bécquer's bedroom was might have given David the wrong idea. Not that it really mattered, yet I found myself blushing.

"Then where is he?" I asked, as sternly as I could manage to hide my embarrassment.

David sighed. "The room next to his study."

It made sense, I thought as I followed him. Yet it saddened me that Bécquer had had to give up the comfort of his own room.

"Would you please let me talk with him first?" David asked as we reached the corridor.

I nodded, somehow relieved. For all my bravado, I was not looking forward to confronting Bécquer. I was afraid, immortal or not, he would be able to see through me, to see how much I cared for him and how distressed I was at his current predicament.

My heart pounding, I leaned against the wall and tried to follow Bécquer's advice on how to block my feelings, while David walked to the door beside the study and knocked twice. There was no answer.

David looked back at me. "I told you he's sleeping," he whispered.

Bécquer, a human Bécquer, would have heard us outside his door. Were he immortal he'd have sensed me coming, even before I'd reached the house. Was he immortal and avoiding me or was he human and sleeping? In either case, I should be leaving. But what if . . . ?

Call me when you see him, Federico had told me.

Ignoring David's attempts to stop me, I grabbed the knob and pushed the door open.

Bécquer was sitting on his bed, propped against a pillow. Despite the darkness inside, I could tell he was wearing the dark shirt he had worn in the afternoon. Thus, I guessed, he was still fully dressed, although I couldn't tell for sure because a dark comforter up to his waist concealed his legs. His arms fell lifeless by his side and, once I got closer, I saw his eyes were closed.

I called his name and, when he didn't react, I took one of his hands in mine, and repeated his name louder and louder, until I was screaming.

"Ms. Esteban!"

David was by my side, pulling at my arm. I pushed him hard to free myself, and leaning over Bécquer, I shook him by his shoulders.

Again, David pulled me back. "Please, let me handle this."

I turned. "What happened? What's wrong with him?"

David picked up a prescription bottle from the bedspread, and showed it to me. "Sleeping pills," he said, pointing at the label. "He took them all," he added when shaking the bottle failed to produce a sound.

I gasped. "You left the pills within his reach?"

"Please move. I need to force him to get rid of them."

David's voice was calm where mine had been frantic and when I looked up at him, ready to argue, I met not the eyes of the careless boy I had found playing video games, but the pragmatic stare of a professional nurse.

"Call 9-1-1 and tell them what happened," David prompted me. "Ask them to send an ambulance at once."

He had unbuttoned Bécquer's shirt while he talked and checked for a pulse on his neck where the scar from Beatriz's vicious attack was still visible. Bécquer's face was gaunt, his breathing, if he was breathing, too shallow for me to notice. Was he alive? Or were we already too late?

Fighting the panic that threatened to engulf me, I grabbed the phone from the bedside table and made the call.

Chapter Seventeen: Bécquer's Letter

By the time the paramedics arrived, Bécquer was still unconscious, but at least his breathing was regular. David had forced him to empty his stomach. Whether we had gotten all the pills from his system in time was too early to say, we were told. Without further reassurance, we were asked to move aside while they connected the IV to his arm, transferred him to a stretcher, and hurried him to the ambulance.

When they told us only one person was allowed to drive with him, David nodded to me. "You go. I've done all I can. Besides, I've to get things ready here before Mr. Bécquer comes home."

I doubted that would happen that night, but David felt it was his responsibility to clean up before the ten o'clock shift arrived. At least, that is what he told me. My guess was that allowing me to go with Bécquer was his way of thanking me for agreeing not to tell his employer he had been playing games when I came in.

Like Federico, I believed that if Bécquer wanted to die, he would have found a way. David did not know about the pills, he'd told me, and he had reacted well to the emergency. Guessing that Bécquer would not have wanted David punished for his decision, I chose not to say anything that could incriminate him.

Chris, the paramedic who was to ride with us, helped me into the back of the ambulance then motioned me to sit by Bécquer. I had barely done so when the strident sound of the siren broke into the night, drowning the roar of the engines as the vehicle started.

Despite David's efforts, Bécquer had never been totally conscious back at the house. But now he opened his eyes.

"Bécquer," I whispered and leaned closer in order to hear him over the blaring of the siren.

He stared at me for a moment then frowned. "Carla?" His voice was hoarse, almost inaudible. "What are you doing here?"

He tried to sit as he spoke, but his arms gave way and he fell back. "Don't move."

Bécquer moaned. "What happened? Where am I?"

"There was an accident. We're taking you to the hospital."

"An accident?" For a moment he looked confused then, as understanding dawned in his eyes, he grabbed the tubing from the IV and yanked it from his arm.

Immediately Chris was upon him. Bécquer fought back with energy I didn't imagine he could have. But the fight didn't last long. Soon, the paramedic had him restrained and bound to the stretcher. Once the IV was again dripping in his arm, Chris moved back.

"Don't get him excited," he told me, as if I were the one responsible for Bécquer's reaction. But seeing no point in arguing, I nodded and sat again by Bécquer's side.

"You have to help me," Bécquer asked me in Spanish now, to keep the paramedic from following our conversation, I guessed. "I was supposed to die tonight."

"I won't let you die."

"Carla, please, don't make this more difficult for me. I can't live. I don't want to live."

"I'm sorry, Bécquer. I'm so sorry."

"So you know?"

"Richard told me."

"Richard? Oh! You mean he told you about my legs?"

I nodded. "Is it true, Bécquer? Are you human?"

He didn't deny it. He just stared at me with his dark eyes that seemed even darker now, sunk so deep in his gaunt face.

"The Elders . . . " I hesitated, "did they make you human?"

"Yes. My punishment for making Beatriz immortal."

"But you didn't change her. She stole your blood."

"That's a technicality, Carla. I sired her, and the sentence was that I should die. I begged Cesar, the Elder's messenger, for a week to finish your contract. And when he agreed he asked for my word that after the week was over I'd kill myself. So, you see, I've no choice."

"Yes, you have," I bluffed. "Federico will talk to the Elders. He will convince them to change their sentence."

"Federico knows?"

"He's coming tonight."

Bécquer groaned. "Why did you tell him? There's nothing he can do. The Elders have already decided. You must let me be."

I shook my head. "I won't."

"Why not? You broke your contract with me today. You were not to see me again. What difference does it make to you whether I live or die?"

"I ended my contract with you to keep my children safe. I don't want you to die."

"Do you hate me so much that you want me to live like this, broken and impotent, a shadow of the god I was?"

"You cannot really mean that. You're still you, Bécquer. No matter what has happened. Taking your life is selfish."

"Selfish?"

"Yes, selfish. Are you really so blind that you don't know you have friends who care for you and would be devastated were you to die?"

"Do I really?"

"Don't tell me you don't know that Richard is totally smitten with you. He's certain your clients will wait if you decided to take a break. And Federico is worried sick about you. And Ryan looks up to you. You can't let him down."

Bécquer closed his eyes while I rambled on, as if embarrassed by my barely concealed distress. He opened them when I finished and fixed his dark stare on me.

"And you?" he whispered. "If I die, would you mourn me for a day?"

My vision blurred by tears. I was still struggling to find my voice when the ambulance came to a stop, and Chris asked me to move aside.

Powerless I watched, as they wheeled Bécquer away.

*

Rachel was talking with the receptionist when I came into the hospital.

Even though Richard had insisted that Rachel and Bécquer were not in a relationship, her distressed behavior that afternoon and her already being at the hospital seemed to suggest otherwise. Yet, on the list of people who cared for Bécquer that I had just enumerated for him I had forgotten to mention her. A simple mistake or an unconscious wish that Richard was right?

The girl turned from the desk as I came in, and as our eyes met, she rushed to my side. She was wearing a short plaid parka over tight black jeans, a yellow scarf around her neck. In her perfectly made-up face, her eyes were no longer red, but the tension was clear in her voice as she asked, "Where is Bécquer? Will he be all right?"

Her face relaxed a little when I told her Bécquer had been conscious when I left him.

"David called me," she explained as we walked to the waiting area.

I had guessed that much.

"So, he's conscious," she repeated when we sat facing each other in a corner of an almost empty waiting room. "That's a good sign, isn't it? He'll recover."

"Yes. But . . . " I couldn't tell her Bécquer's life was still in jeopardy because the Elders wanted him dead. Not without learning first how much she knew. "He seems depressed," I continued watching for her reaction. "Not surprising, of course, given his recent prognosis after the accident."

"It was not an accident." Rachel's voice that had been subdued before was now so loud several of the people scattered around the room looked up. "A man came to see Bécquer last Monday," she continued in a lower tone. "A man, tall and dark. 'Cesar,' he said, when I asked him for his name. He didn't wait for me to announce his arrival. As soon as I let him in, he dashed past me to Bécquer's study as if he owned the house. So I assumed they were friends. But I was wrong. Bécquer was not happy to see him, that much was clear, although he smiled at me and told me I could take the afternoon off."

"I thought it was you who found Bécquer."

"I did," Rachel said, her eyes somewhat unfocused. "I didn't leave as he asked me to. Cesar made me uncomfortable, and I didn't want Bécquer to be alone with him. So I waited. And waited. But he never came out of Bécquer's study. When I gathered my courage and knocked at the door, nobody answered, so I went in. Bécquer was unconscious on the floor and Cesar was gone.

"Bécquer told the doctors he had fallen down the stairs, but that is impossible. He was nowhere near the stairs when I found him. I think Bécquer and Cesar fought and Cesar is responsible for his condition."

"You don't believe me?" Rachel asked when I said nothing. "I knew you wouldn't. That's why I brought this." She reached into a canvas bag hanging from the back of her chair and produced a manila envelope. "Bécquer gave me this in the morning and asked me to mail it to you, even though you were coming in the afternoon."

"It's addressed to you," she explained as I frowned. "My guess is that he wrote to you to explain what happened."

I took the envelope she offered. Inside I found a leather-bound journal filled with Bécquer's florid handwriting. A letter-size envelope was concealed among its pages.

My heart beating hard, I tore open the envelope, unfolded the letter, and started reading.

Dear Carla,

I'm writing this letter as I wait for you to come. When you read it, I'll be dead.

Cesar, one of the Elders, came last Monday. His orders were to kill me, but I pleaded with him to let me live for a week longer so that I could finish my contract with you. He agreed after I promised I would take my own life afterward. As a precaution, he made me mortal and severed my spine so I would not escape.

Once I'm gone, the Elders will destroy any shred of evidence that would reveal their or my own existence as an immortal. I abided by their desires when I was first changed. I told my friends to burn my old journals and the letters to my brother where I mentioned my secret life, and I would have done the same today, except that, if I do, you would forget me. I'm fool enough to believe you care for me just a little, just enough to want to know who I really was.

Please believe me when I say I didn't kill myself out of despair, nor because I am a coward and don't want to face life in my present condition. I did it only because I promised Cesar I would do so.

My mortality has returned to me the gift of writing. Reason enough to make me want to live this mortal life. The other reason, I suppose you've already guessed, it's you.

Alas, the choice has been taken from me, and so I will die tonight. But in my last act of defiance, I'm sending you this diary. Read it or burn it, as you please. But know, in either case, that my main regret as I prepare to die is that I did not have more time to be with you.

Goodbye Carla. I hope that, despite my many faults, you will remember me. And if you, I dare not hope, were to love me in return, know I will remain with you forever, made immortal by your love.

Gustavo Adolfo Bécquer

"Does he mention Cesar?"

Rachel's voice startled me, bringing me back to the hospital room. I nodded. "Yes, Cesar caused his 'accident' last Monday."

"Then we have to tell the police. He must pay for what he did."

"No. I don't think we should interfere. The decision must be Bécquer's."

Rachel hesitated.

"Please wait, at least until we talk to him. There is no last name in the letter. No way to trace this Cesar, or prove he's real. It's our word against Bécquer's."

"And the notebook?" she said pointing at Bécquer's diary sitting on my lap. "Maybe he tells more about Cesar there."

I knew the diary would not help us locate Cesar either because Cesar was an immortal, thus beyond human reach. Yet, curious to know what Bécquer had written, I opened it to the first page.

I was eleven when I met Lucrezia on the patio of my aunt's house. The year was 1847 and Sevilla was in spring, but not my heart, for my heart was still frozen in the winter morning, two months past, that had seen my mother die.

"She's in heaven," the priest had said, "because God had need of her."

I nodded at him in fake assent, for the fear of the Church had been ingrained in me from the time I was a little boy and I knew better than to argue with my betters. But whatever need God had of Mother, I thought it was selfish of Him to take her from me and my seven brothers; God had the whole world to choose from and He had already taken Father from us.

Overwhelmed by my loss and unable to sleep, I took to wandering the silent house in the dark of night. My aunt's house, like most houses in Sevilla at the time, was built around a patio, its walls washed white, an orange tree on a corner and in the middle a running fountain to help fight the unbearable heat that came with summer. And it was sitting on the low ridge of the stone basin I saw Lucrezia for the first time.

Bécquer's words jumped at me from the page, kidnapping me

against my will. I'd have continued reading, oblivious to Rachel and my foreign surroundings, if her voice had not interrupted me.

"Does he say who this Cesar is?"

I put the notebook down and, feeling strangely conscious as if I had been found peering through the window into somebody's home, I shook my head. "No, he doesn't. I don't think we'll find any clue about Cesar here."

"Why?"

"It's just a story. I think Bécquer meant for me to have it only after his death. I'm not sure I should read it while he's still alive."

"And is he? Is Bécquer alive?"

I looked up, startled by the familiar and unexpected voice.

From his six feet of height, Ryan looked down at me.

Chapter Eighteen: In the Hospital

"Ryan?" I half stood then sat back again, worn down by my son's scowl. "What are you doing here?"

"Never mind that," Ryan said, his voice cold. "Tell me about Bécquer."

"The doctors are with him now. But how did you—?"

"Madison told me you were at Bécquer's. I thought it would be a good time to confront you two together and try to change your mind about my not seeing him, so I went there. David told me what happened.

"I'm going to see him," he added lowering his lanky frame in the chair across from us. "Don't try to stop me."

"I won't, Ryan. I think it would be good for him to see that you care."

Ryan scowled as if ready to argue then frowned. "You mean you're all right with that?"

"Yes, Ryan." Turning toward the girl sitting by my side, I added, "And this is Rachel, by the way."

Ryan looked at Rachel, as if he had just realized she was there, which knowing him, he probably had. Bending forward, he extended his hand to her. "I'm Ryan," he said, reverting to his usual charming self. But when he turned to me, his voice was cold again. "It's your fault. You know that, right?"

"Ryan, please. I wasn't even there."

"It's your fault because you didn't let me see him. If I had, I would have noticed Bécquer was depressed. I would have helped him."

"It's not so simple. Bécquer—"

"—can't walk. I know. David told me. But you didn't. Why didn't you tell me?"

"Don't blame your mother," Rachel said before I could answer. "I was with him every day this past week, and he never seemed depressed to me. So, actually, if someone is to blame it would be me."

"Of course not," Ryan told her. "How could you have known?"

By the eagerness of his voice, I knew the irony of his statement was lost on him.

"Thanks." Rachel frowned, as her eyes focused on his face. "I know you, I think. Aren't you the second guitar from Shut Up and Listen?"

"I am." Ryan smiled, obviously pleased at being recognized. "Or was, I guess. I'm not sure if the band will hold together now that Matt's gone."

"Why not? You could take his place as leader."

Ryan beamed at the girl.

His anger at me momentarily forgotten, he plunged into a technical discussion of his possible suitability for the job while Rachel smiled at him. Relieved at the respite this turn of the conversation provided, I slid Bécquer's notebook and letter in my handbag and grabbed my phone.

I had called Federico from Bécquer's house and, when I got no answer, left a message on his voice mail. He had not called me back. Or maybe he had, I thought as I realized my phone was dead. I threw it back in my purse and asked Ryan to lend me his.

"Why?" Ryan snapped.

Because I'm asking, I wanted to say, but that would have gotten us nowhere. "Because Federico and Matt are driving back tonight to be with Bécquer," I said instead, "and they don't know he's here."

Without a word, he took his cell phone from his pocket and handed it to me.

I was punching Federico's number when the doors to the ER swung open and a nurse came through. I froze and watched as, after a brief interchange with the receptionist, she started toward the area where we were sitting. The three of us stood as one.

"How is he?" I asked, after the nurse confirmed we were waiting for him.

"His vitals are stable," she informed us in a professional voice. "But we want to keep him through the night for observation."

"I want to see him," Ryan said.

"I'm afraid that won't be possible." The nurse's tone became imperious. "He has requested to be left alone. So you'll have to wait until morning."

He's planning to do it again, I thought while Ryan insisted. "Bécquer doesn't know I'm here. He would see me if he knew. I'm his nephew."

The nurse shook her head, her annoyance unmistakable now. "Not tonight."

I grabbed Ryan's arm and pulled at him, afraid that if he continued pressing the nurse with his demands, he would ruin not only his, but also my chance of seeing Bécquer.

"It's all right, Ryan. You'll see him tomorrow," I coaxed him.

He was about to argue when Rachel set her hand on his other arm. "Come on, Ryan. Your mother's right. Let's go. You can come back early in the morning."

Ryan hesitated for a moment then nodded at Rachel and shaking himself free of my grasp, moved back.

I asked the nurse for more details about Bécquer's condition while I waited for Rachel and Ryan to reach the exit doors. Then I steered the conversation back to the issue of seeing Bécquer.

"I won't bother him," I told her, trying to keep the anxiety from my voice. "But I would very much like to stay in the room with him tonight." As she shook her head, I rushed in, "You must let me stay with him. He'll try to kill himself again. He admitted that much to me."

A flash of anger crossed the nurse's eyes. "I assure you your brother will not hurt himself here. In this hospital, we observe the highest standards of safety."

Turning her back on me, she disappeared through the swinging doors.

"He's not my brother," I said to no one in particular as I watched the door swing, alternately inviting and rejecting me. I considered following her, but glanced at the reception desk and noted the girl had followed our conversation and was watching me.

Frustrated, I went back to my seat and considered my possibilities. Going home was out of the question. Whatever high standards the hospital had, I knew Bécquer was not safe. I would wait for another nurse to come by and ask her to be taken to his room. In the meantime, I would pray the haughty nurse was right.

Lucky for me, Ryan had forgotten to ask for his phone back. This time Federico answered on the first ring.

"He got it wrong," he said after I repeated what Bécquer had told me during the ambulance ride. "I just talked with the Elders. Their sentence was to make him human. 'A life for a life,' that is how they phrased it. He will die eventually, of course, as all humans do, but the messenger was not supposed to kill him. He's not supposed to be paralyzed either."

"Bécquer said that Cesar did it so he could not flee."

Federico swore. "Cesar? No wonder. I should have guessed."

"Guessed what?"

"Cesar hates Bécquer. So he obviously twisted the Elders' words to push Bécquer to kill himself, then paralyzed him just for his enjoyment. It fits just perfectly with his treacherous mind. His immortality has only increased the thirst for blood and depravity that made him infamous when he was human."

"Who was he as human?"

"His last name was Borgia. He was Cesar Borgia. The one who inspired Machiavelli to write *The Prince*. The bastard son of that other Alexander, the Renaissance pope who ruled the Church with the libertinism and nepotism of an absolute king."

"Oh!" I said. For what else can you say when history, the history you studied at school becomes alive on a Saturday evening in, of all unlikely places, the waiting room of a hospital?

"Listen, Carla. I have to hang up now. I need to talk with the Elders again. They forbade me to help Bécquer before, claiming that his paralysis had happened after he became human. But if Cesar caused it—"

"Then you can heal him?"

"I hope so. As I hope they will send somebody to talk to Bécquer. He needs to explain to them that Beatriz stole his blood for they believe he changed her on purpose. Once this point is clarified, they may even revert their sentence. In the meantime, you keep Bécquer safe, all right?"

"Of course," I said, as if I could.

A thousand times more eager to see Bécquer now that I knew the Elders did not want him dead for I hoped knowing this would stop him from trying to kill himself, I walked to the desk. Unlike the nurse, the receptionist seemed sympathetic to my request, or maybe she was just bored and glad to have something to do.

"I'll check with the nurse," she told me.

She punched a number on the phone and conveyed my request. "I'll tell her," she said shortly.

"What is wrong?" I asked prompted by the note of concern I had noticed in her voice.

"Probably nothing," she said lightly, but her eyes did not mine as she gestured toward the elevator. "They want you upstairs. Third floor. A nurse will meet you there."

Too impatient to wait for the elevator, I ran up the stairs, arriving at the third floor flushed and out of breath. But it was fear, and not the running, that made my heart pump faster.

The nurse who had talked with us before was waiting for me by the elevator. Her haughty look, I noticed, was gone.

"I apologize," she said when I joined her. "You were right, about your brother. He tried again."

"Did he? Is he—"

"He's all right. We got him in time. But I believe it would be better if you stayed with him."

"Did he swallow more pills?" I asked as I followed her down the corridor.

"No. He charmed one of the nurses into bringing him flowers. We always have extras from the maternity ward. New parents are too busy with their babies to carry all the bouquets they get. He smashed the vase and tried to cut his wrist with the broken glass.

"You have to give him points for ingenuity," she continued. But the image her words evoked of the blood spilling from Bécquer's veins was vivid in my mind that I felt dizzy, and for a moment I saw black.

"Are you all right?"

I opened my eyes. The nurse had grabbed my arm. I was glad she had, because my knees had grown weak. I took a deep breath. "Yes, of course."

"He's not your brother, is he?"

I shook my head. "No. He's not."

"I didn't think so." I blushed—was my attraction to him so obvious?—"He was pretty vocal about not having any sisters. And also about not wanting anybody with him."

"Yet, you let me come," I said as we resumed walking.

Her smile disappeared. "In my experience, a suicide attempt is a cry for help. A disability is tough on a relationship. Until he has come to accept his condition, my advice is that you tell him that you love him. Unconditionally."

As I struggled with my reply, she stopped and knocked briefly on a closed door and, without waiting for a response, entered the room.

Chapter Nineteen: The Pact

Bécquer was lying back on a half-raised bed. His hair, tousled and matted with sweat, framed a face so white it could have been a sculpture.

I stood by the door, not sure how to proceed while the nurse checked his IV and took his vitals. Ignoring her, Bécquer stared at me with his dark, sunken eyes. Still totally still, and silent. That he was still was not surprising as his arms, set parallel to his body, were strapped to the bed. The silence he broke at last, when the nurse left closing the door. Polite and distant, he thanked me for coming and asked me to take a seat next to his bed.

"So, it's you," he said when I did. "The mysterious sister I never had."

Afraid my voice would break if I spoke, I only nodded. His wrists, I noticed as I looked down to avoid his stare, were bandaged.

"Is that how you think of me?" he continued. "As the brother you must keep from harm?"

I swallowed hard. "Ryan claimed to be your nephew. The nurse assumed—"

"Ryan is here?"

He struggled to sit up as he spoke, the muscles on his naked arms flexed under the straps binding him to the bed.

"Please don't let him come," he said as, defeated, he fell back. "I don't want him to see me like this."

You should have thought of that before, I thought. But he looked so hurt and dejected I couldn't bring myself to say it.

"He left already," I said instead. "When the nurse told him he couldn't see you until tomorrow."

Bécquer sighed in relief, then again his face tightened. "Does he think I'm a coward?"

"No. He blames me."

"You?" Bécquer frowned, then nodded when I told him why. "I'll talk to him."

"Of course, you will," I said, frustration and despair spilling into my voice. "And when do you plan to do that, before or after you kill yourself?"

"Touché. I'm sorry, Carla. I really am. But I told you, I have no choice."

"Yes, you have. Federico spoke to the Elders tonight. Cesar lied to you. The Elders sentenced you to be human, not to death. To be human, not paralyzed."

He closed his eyes.

I touched his hand with my fingers. "Bécquer—" I started. Whatever I was about to tell him I forgot when I met his eyes for there was so much hope in them. So much despair. I leaned down and kissed his lips.

Bécquer did not respond. I moved back.

"Don't play with me, Carla." His voice was cold. His face unreadable.

"I'm not playing."

"I overheard the nurse talking to you. I heard her asking you to pretend you love me."

"You think my kiss was a lie?"

Bécquer said nothing.

"You're wrong, Bécquer. Besides, what the nurse said does not apply anymore. You will not be paralyzed for long. Nor human for that matter. Once you tell the Elders what really happened the day Beatriz became immortal, Federico is certain the Elders will reverse your sentence."

"They won't. Because I did change her, and I'm taking full responsibility for it."

I frowned. "But that's not true. Why should you—"

Bécquer's face hardened into a mask, but for a brief moment his eyes met mine, and, as they did, an image jumped to my conscious mind: the image of Beatriz holding Ryan over the dam and of Bécquer facing her. And I knew, as clearly as if I had heard their words what the pact between them had been.

"You promised her," I said, and my voice came out broken, almost unrecognizable. "You promised Beatriz you'd take responsibility for her change if she let Ryan go."

It wasn't a question. Had it been, his silence would have been answer enough.

"I cannot, I will not, let you take the blame."

"I'm afraid it's not your decision, Carla. You were not there. You have no proof."

"I may not have proof, but now that you're human you cannot lie to the immortals anymore, for they don't need your permission to read your mind. Federico we'll have no problem learning the truth."

Bécquer swore and I knew I had won because he changed his tactic.

"Carla, you don't understand." His voice that had been hard before was now pleading. "I gave her my word. If I break it, Beatriz will not abide by her promise and Ryan will be in danger again. Not only him, your daughter—"

"Madison," I supplied my daughter's name automatically.

"Madison will be in danger too."

I hesitated for a moment. Fear for my children weighed against my responsibility to make things right for Bécquer.

"I have to tell the truth. I can't let you take the blame for something you didn't do."

"You said your kiss was not a lie, Carla. This is your test. If you care for me you will respect my wish."

"I can't."

"So I was right. You don't care for me. Or maybe you did. You cared for me when I was immortal. Not for this broken human I have become."

"You're wrong."

"Prove it to me then. Stand by me. Don't tell Federico about my pact with Beatriz. Convince him he can't tell the Elders what happened between us."

"But—"

"Carla, listen. I've lived for a long time. Your children haven't. They deserve to live more than I do. Besides, you saved my life. I owe you."

I sighed.

"All right, I'll support your decision."

"Thank you, Carla. So maybe it's true you care for me a little."

His voice was light and teasing and his eyes were asking me to come closer. But I couldn't move. I felt dirty. I had agreed to Bécquer's request in order to save my children's lives, but, deep down, I knew it was wrong. If the Elders knew the truth they would allow Bécquer to be immortal. But if I didn't tell them, he would remain human and, maybe even, paralyzed.

"It's all right." Bécquer said, serious now. "I understand you won't want to stay with me under these circumstances." Briefly, his eyes moved to his legs, then without a hint of self pity, held mine again. "You owe me no explanation."

"Of course I want to stay with you," I said, angry for letting my silence give him the wrong impression. "I love you, Bécquer. Your present circumstances are of no importance to me. I'll stay with you as long as you'll have me."

Bécquer stared at me for a long time. "Do you really mean it?"

"I do."

Bending over, I kissed him again.

This time his lips opened as they touched mine, and, just before I closed my eyes, I saw myself on his black pupils, dark mirrors reflecting my soul as it met his own. His lips were soft and warm, inviting yet demanding, his kiss both pleasure and pain. I wanted to scream and I wanted to die. I wanted this kiss never to end and I wanted to flee for I was scared of losing myself, of forgetting everything I'd ever been, or was, or planned to be. Yet, I didn't mind. I didn't care if I ever had a thought but this: That he was mine and I, his, this moment and every moment. He and I but one, a single soul. Forever.

"Carla" he said when we at last parted. "Could you—?"

"Kiss you once more?"

He smiled. "That too. But first could you untie me?"

I considered his request. They had bound him so he would not kill himself, but now that he knew the Elders didn't want him dead, he wouldn't try again, would he?

"Should I trust you?"

Bécquer smile widened. "I'll be a gentleman. I promise." The mischief he infused into his words, made me believe, at last, that he would fight to stay alive.

Bécquer flexed his arms when I finished, disregarding the UV tubing attached to his left hand.

"Be careful." I reached over the bed to stay the tubing that swung wildly.

Bécquer winced.

"Sorry. Did I hurt you?"

He lay back and shook his head.

But I knew he was lying because his eyes were full of pain. "Seriously, Bécquer, how do you feel?"

Bécquer shrugged. "The truth?"

I nodded.

"If you were not with me," he said, with a deprecatory smile, "I would think I had died and gone to hell."

"Maybe you have," I teased him. "Maybe, like Sartre claimed, *L'enfer c'est les autres*. Hell is other people. And I am yours."

"No. You're not, that I know for certain. Although, once upon a time, my private hell did have a woman's name."

"Lucrezia."

I said the name without thinking, the name of the woman he mentioned in his diary.

Bécquer frowned and, as I blushed under his dark stare, he

sighed. "You read my diary."

"Only the first page. Rachel wanted me to read it to prove Cesar was real, although you had denied it. She thought you might mention him in your diary.

"Did she read it too?"

"No, she didn't."

"Nothing happened between us."

"Rachel or Lucrezia?"

"I meant Rachel. As for Lucrezia—"

"You don't owe me an explanation."

He smiled ruefully. "Come," he asked me and when following his suggestion I sat by his side, he took my hand. "Yes. I have to tell you about Lucrezia. But I fear that when I do, I'll lose your respect. And your love."

"Because you still love her?"

"No, Carla. I don't love her. That's not why. I'm afraid that you'll think poorly of me because I'm ashamed of who I was and how I lived my life when I was human."

"You were Bécquer, when you were human. Gustavo Adolfo Bécquer. How can you be ashamed? You're admired, adored by legions of fans that have read your poetry, your legends, your letters."

Bécquer laughed. "My fans, as you call them, do not love me. They love the myth I created after my death. My so-called death, anyway. During my life, I was an unknown, a failure as a writer, a dilettante of sorts, working clerk jobs I couldn't keep, writing pieces for newspapers, articles nobody read, searching all the time for that elusive perfect nirvana Lucrezia gave me when I was a child."

"So you loved her back then?"

"If you call that love. What I felt for her was more like an addiction, a disease that stole my soul and poisoned my mind. And because in my ignorance I called that love, I spent my life searching for the intangible—a silver moon ray, a pair of green eyes, the impossible I could never have."

"Did Lucrezia love you?"

"I doubt Lucrezia was capable of love. Besides, I was eleven when I met her, a boy still grieving the death of his mother. How could she love me? I was her human pet, nothing more. Later, maybe she coveted my young body and the adoration she saw in my eyes. And so for a while, we were lovers drinking in each other: me in her beauty, she in the glow of my love for her.

"Until one day, she left me, without explanation, without saying goodbye. I spent the rest of my life longing for her, while she in turn took me as her lover or rejected me, only to taunt me again when I fell in love with someone else.

"And, all the time, Cesar watched us—either jealous or amused, I do not know—biding his time to avenge himself for the few moments of bliss Lucrezia gave me."

"Cesar? The same Cesar who ordered you to kill yourself?"

"The very same. Cesar was Lucrezia's lover and her brother. In life and after death."

Of course. Cesar was Cesar Borgia, Federico had told me. Which made Lucrezia the infamously beautiful Lucrezia Borgia.

"Cesar made her immortal against the Elder's wishes," Bécquer explained. "Apart from beauty, she had no merits of her own. She was not artistically, nor scientifically gifted, and thus by the Elder's rules, she did not qualify to become immortal. But Alexander, the Elders' leader, loved Cesar at the time and allowed Cesar's defiance to go unchallenged. Eventually Alexander moved on to other lovers, and Cesar continued his affair with Lucrezia. They were still together when I met her in Sevilla."

"Is that why he hates you? Because once upon a time you and Lucrezia were lovers?"

"He hates me because Lucrezia made me an immortal against his wishes and, in his wrath at her defiance, Cesar killed her. He blames me for his actions."

"If you knew he hates you, how could you believe him when he told you the Elders had sentenced you to death?"

"He believed me because I said the truth," A deep, sarcastic voice answered from the door.

Letting go of my hands, Bécquer leaned forward, his body tense as if preparing for a fight. A fight he couldn't win, even if he were not bedridden, because the man standing by the door, dark and beautiful like an angel fallen from grace, was Cesar.

And Cesar was immortal.

Chapter Twenty: Cesar

"The Elders want you dead," the man said in heavily accented English as he stepped into the room. "I should know for I am one of them."

"You want me dead, Cesar, not the Elders. Their sentence was to make me mortal."

"And so you are, my dear Gustavo, quite mortal indeed. Unfortunately, mortals have a nasty habit of dying and so it is that a sentence to be mortal is equivalent, in my opinion, to one of death."

With a speed that would have betrayed him as being immortal had I not already known, Cesar reached his side then turned to me. "But I see you have company," he said, appraising me. "Aren't you going to introduce us?"

"You must leave." Where Cesar's voice had been sarcastic, Bécquer's was cold. "The Elders are aware that you manipulated me, bending their sentence with your lies so I would agree to end my life. If I die today, they will hold you responsible. And if you hurt Carla, I will haunt you for all eternity."

Cesar laughed. "Would you really haunt me for all eternity? How poetic. But, of course, you always had a way with words. While I was more of a man of action. As for your lady, Carla did you say?" He turned again to me. "I'm Cesar. Cesar Borgia, at your service."

Grabbing my hand, he bent to kiss it. The chivalrous gesture an ominous sign, a warning that he set the rules.

Bécquer swore and yanked the IV tubing from his arm. I held my breath, expecting the alarm to go off. But it didn't. The numbers in the machine were frozen, which meant we had once more stepped out of time. Nobody would come to help us now. Which really made no difference as no human would stand a chance against an immortal. At the thought, the fear inside me grew exponentially.

Unlike me, Bécquer didn't seem surprised when his action had no effect. His eyes on Cesar, he ordered him to leave once more.

Cesar nodded. "I will," he said as if he meant it. "As soon as you confirm that you'll keep your promise to take your own life before Monday."

"I won't. You lied to me, Cesar, which means my word is not binding, for it was given under a false premise."

"Isn't it?" A triumphant smile curved Cesar's pale lips as he turned toward the door. "Now you believe me? Now you believe your reluctant sire is an oath breaker?"

At Cesar's words, a second visitor materialized by the door. It was Beatriz, I realized, as she glided forward and came to stand by Bécquer's side.

I took a step back for nothing human remained in her face, the beautiful face of a vengeful goddess. But Bécquer, unperturbed as though he had expected her, returned her stare.

Gracefully, Beatriz sat on his bed and bent forward until their faces almost touched. When she spoke, her perfectly modulated voice was that of a lover. But her words were not of love.

"And what excuse do you have to break the oath you gave to me?" she asked him.

"I did not break my oath to you." Bécquer's voice was even and, although not loud, it broke the intimacy she had established between them. And so it was Cesar who answered. "No. You didn't. You sent your lap dog to do it in your stead."

"Is that so?" Beatriz asked.

"No," Bécquer said. "I did not send Federico."

"Liar." Cupping Bécquer's face in her hands, Beatriz forced him to look at her. Bécquer's eyes turned vacant under her stare, then his arms grew limp.

"Stop it! He's telling the truth."

I reached for her as I screamed. Without looking, Beatriz swung her right arm and hit me hard on the chest, sending me crashing to the floor.

Fighting the blackness that threatened to engulf me, I opened my eyes. Cesar was looking down on me, his hand extended. He shrugged when I refused it and watched as I scrambled to my feet.

"No. You didn't tell Federico." Beatriz released Bécquer, who fell back against the pillow. Blinking repeatedly, Bécquer sat up. A sigh of relief escaped his lips when he met my eyes.

"You didn't tell him," Beatriz repeated staring at me. "But you told her."

"He didn't. I guessed it on my own." I took a step forward, but Cesar grabbed my arm, holding me back.

Ignoring me, Beatriz bent over Bécquer and pinned him to the bed. "What else did you tell her?" she whispered, her voice tense with hate. "Did you tell her that you loved her?"

"Let Carla go," Bécquer said, addressing Cesar. "She has nothing to do with us."

"You're right. She hasn't. But I can't let her go. She knows too much."

"Cesar is right," Beatriz added. "And anyway, why would you care what is to become of her?"

"Oh, I see," she continued when he said nothing. "You think you're in love with her, don't you?" She laughed. "You are pathetic. After all the women you have seduced over the years, after all your broken promises, you still believe you are capable of love?"

"Come on, Beatriz. Kill him already. We're wasting time." Cesar sounded bored.

"Don't listen to him," Bécquer spoke, his voice even. "I have told the Elders that I changed you, as I promised, so they will let you live. But if you kill me—"

"What about her?" Beatriz asked. "Will she lie for me too?"

No, the answer came to my mind unbidden. Anger spilling over the walls I was trying to erect to keep Beatriz from reading my feelings.

Remember, it was you who condemned him. As her voice yelled in my mind, she bent over Bécquer and sank her long canines into his unprotected neck.

I screamed and fought the tight grip of Cesar's arms around me. As if in answer to my plea, the loud, jarring playing of an electric guitar filled the room, drowning my cries and Cesar's laughter.

Beatriz looked up toward the chair, toward the sound of Ryan's phone coming from my handbag. Bécquer's arm shot forward and struck her neck. As her blood splattered over the white sheets, he drew her to him.

Releasing me, Cesar bolted and pulled Beatriz from Bécquer.

Her hands clapping her neck where blood still poured out, Beatriz staggered against the chair where she collapsed.

Sitting up, Bécquer challenged Cesar with his stare. In his hands, he held a shard of glass stained in blood. A piece of the vase he must have hidden before the nurses came to stop his last attempt to end his life.

Cesar laughed. "A piece of glass? Do you really think you can stop me with that, you pathetic mortal?"

His arm lashed as he spoke. But Bécquer blocked his attack and when Cesar moved back, his hand was bleeding.

Cesar swore. "You bastard. You drank from her."

Bécquer said nothing. On his face, as pale as marble, only his eyes seemed alive, intent on Cesar. One moment passed, then his arm shook, and I knew his strength was wavering.

I called to Cesar to distract him and rushed toward Bécquer. But before I could reach him, I felt the pressure of Cesar's mind on mine, willing me to stop. Unable to move, I watched as Cesar grabbed Bécquer's arm. I heard the cracking sound of the bone breaking, and then saw Bécquer's hand open, releasing the shard.

Cesar snarled. "Tell me Bécquer, do you prefer to die now or should I kill your ladylove first?"

Cradling his broken arm, Bécquer said nothing.

"This is not how it was supposed to be." Cesar pointed at Beatriz, who was slumped on the chair, unconscious or dead I was not sure. "She was supposed to kill you."

"Let me guess," Bécquer said, the effort to speak showing in the way his words came out, one by one and broken. "You will kill me now, but she will take the blame when you tell the Elders. In your version, Beatriz attacked me. You tried to stop her but were too late to save me, and in the fight that ensued, you killed Beatriz unwillingly. A dead Beatriz suits you fine because, dead, she cannot confess she stole my blood or that it was you who asked her to kill me."

"Precisely."

Cesar raised his arm once more, his flat hand a mortal weapon aimed at Bécquer's chest, and I could do nothing but watch and wait for the fatal blow that would stop his heart. Only it never happened because someone else entered the room, too fast for me to see, and grabbed Cesar's arm as it struck.

Cesar turned. His eyes widened when he saw the man holding him. "Alexander," he said, his voice slightly off.

"You have disobeyed our orders," the man said, "thus you will answer to us now."

The metallic edge of his voice broke the wall that immobilized me. Barely aware of the two immortals dressed in black who had materialized in the room and were carrying Cesar away, I ran to Bécquer's side calling his name. But Bécquer, pale and still, didn't stir.

"Bécquer is not dead," Alexander's voice came from behind. "Just unconscious."

I turned. Over his shoulder, I saw two different men, also in black, carrying Beatriz out of the room. Cesar was nowhere in sight.

"You must leave now, Carla," Alexander said, not unkindly.

I didn't move. "You saved Bécquer's life, and I'm grateful. But I won't leave him."

"You must," he insisted and his voice had the authority of an ancient king's. "Bécquer's sentence has been revoked for we are aware that Beatriz stole Bécquer's blood. He's safe with us."

With the uncanny speed immortals moved, he rushed by me.

Sitting by Bécquer's side, grabbed his broken arm, and snapped the bone in place. Then he bent over and kissed him on the lips.

He's changing him. He's making him an immortal. The thought startled me. If Bécquer became an immortal, I could not be with him, I could not even talk to him because I wouldn't trust him.

I jumped forward. "No."

I grabbed Alexander's arm. A lame attempt on my part, for his muscles felt like iron under my hand. Yet Alexander did stop and turned to face me. The drop of blood glowing bright red on his lips confirmed my suspicion.

"May I talk with him first?" My voice, weak with wanting, was barely audible.

Alexander shook his head. "I wouldn't recommend waking him up. His body is healing too fast for a mortal's consciousness to endure."

"So, he's mortal still?"

"For now. But if you excuse me—"

"Please, don't."

"Why not?"

"Because . . . " Desperate, I looked around, and my eyes met the machine that was supposed to read Bécquer's vitals but that was now frozen displaying the numbers of its last reading. The numbers of a mortal Bécquer. What would they read, I wondered, after he was no longer human? And that gave me the answer I was looking for. "Because if you do, Bécquer would be miraculously healed by morning and that would have the doctors wondering."

Alexander laughed. "They won't ask any questions, believe me. I will see to it."

If I had considered seeing Bécquer after his change, Alexander's casual acceptance that he manipulated humans' minds reaffirmed my decision to stay away from immortals. If I wanted to say goodbye to Bécquer, the only way to do so was to postpone his change.

"What about the charts," I improvised, "the medical records?" Had any immortal ever been at the hospital? Did the Elders have a protocol to deal with a situation such as this one?

Apparently not, because for the first time Alexander hesitated. "It could be arranged for new records to be made. But maybe it would be better if we wait to change him until he's home."

His eyes narrowed on me. "Talking to Bécquer will change nothing," he said, his words confirming my suspicion that he had sensed my feelings. "Bécquer will choose to be immortal."

"I only want to say goodbye while he is still human."

"I'll let him know. But you must promise you won't wake him up tonight."

I swallowed hard. "I promise."

"All right, then. I'll leave now. When Federico comes, tell him we'll reconvene at Bécquer's house by noon tomorrow."

I nodded, a useless gesture because Alexander was already gone. The pressing beeping of the machine announcing it had been disconnected told me time had resumed its course for us.

Soon a nurse came in—the night nurse I had not met before. I told her Bécquer had broken his arm struggling against the straps that bound him to his bed. The fact that she didn't question the unlikeness of my explanation, nor argue when I told her he didn't need a cast, just to have his arm set, made me guess Alexander was controlling her mind.

When Federico arrived later that night, Bécquer was still unconscious. The immortal blood healing his body had raised his temperature so that his skin was hot to the touch, and the few times he opened his eyes, he had not recognized me. But Federico reassured me Bécquer would be better by morning.

"You should go now," he insisted. "You shouldn't be present when I talk to them."

He didn't explain further and I didn't ask. Instead, I asked him to tell Bécquer that I wanted to talk with him before he became immortal.

Federico promised and, out of excuses to stay, I left.

I left, reluctantly, because I knew quite well as I closed the door that Bécquer would be immortal the next day and I would never see him again.

It hurt to walk.

Chapter Twenty-One: Red Roses

I called Ryan from the hospital. He was home, I knew, because he had left a voice message before, telling me so and demanding to know whether I had stayed at the hospital. For once, I didn't resent his challenging me, because his call had distracted Beatriz and saved Bécquer's life and mine.

It was after midnight by the time Ryan arrived to pick me up. Exhausted physically and mentally, I wanted nothing more than to go home. But my car was at Bécquer's and if I didn't retrieve it now, I risked running into the Elders the next day. I didn't want to meet the Elders nor Bécquer unless he asked for me before being turned immortal. I had no choice but to get the car now.

Ryan frowned when I asked him to drive me to Bécquer's house. "We can go together to see him tomorrow. Your car will be safe there till then."

I shook my head. "I'd rather go now."

"Why?"

I recognized the tension in his voice, a clear warning that he was ready to fight were I to forbid him to see Bécquer. I was too tired to argue with him. So I didn't. I didn't tell him he couldn't see Bécquer. I told him the truth instead.

Yes, I still believed any relationship between humans and immortals was unwise, dangerous even, but Ryan was eighteen, no longer a baby for me to cradle and protect. And if I couldn't stop him from seeing Bécquer, I owed him the truth so he could make a more informed decision on his own. So, on the way to Bécquer's house, I told him what I knew about the immortals.

"You don't expect me to believe that, do you?" Ryan asked me when I finished.

I shrugged. "It's the truth."

"It's absurd." With the same determination he had shown at six when he argued that Santa Claus did not exist, he argued now that immortals did not, could not be. But the very fact that he was arguing told me a part of him believed already. The part that questioned my explanation of what had happened when Beatriz kidnapped him on Halloween.

By the time we reached Bécquer's house, he had run out of questions.

"Drive safe," I told him as he stopped the car. Ryan didn't answer and when I bent to kiss him, he withdrew his face from me. By the time I reached my car, the screech of tires on gravel had faded away.

*

Bécquer didn't call the next day, or the following, and my hope of seeing him before he became immortal dissipated as the days passed. On Tuesday, when I was certain he would not call, I took his diary out of the envelope and read it in one sitting. Based on the dates of his entries, he had written it the previous week, when he was human.

It was the Bécquer of his *Rhymes and Legends*, the one who came through his writing, a Bécquer curious and naive, and terribly romantic. In his unaffected style, he described his obsession with Lucrezia, his love for Julia—the girl Cesar drove away from him with lies, and later married—his acceptance of a marriage of convenience with Casta, imposed on them by her father's knowledge of the immortals and his threat to expose Bécquer to the Bishop. Bécquer had accepted mainly out of hope that a marriage blessed by the Church would put an end to his curse. He was wrong: his attraction to Lucrezia did not go away, but with time, Bécquer grew fond of his wife and very much in love with his children, including Emilio, my ancestor.

His love for this baby who was not his and must have been for him a constant reminder of his failure as a husband, underscored a gentleness of his character that only enhanced my feelings for him. Feelings I knew I had to push out of my mind for Bécquer was immortal once more, and I could not see him again.

Although it hurt, I had to accept that Bécquer was gone from my life. The only palpable proof he had ever existed was my two-book deal and the name of an agent I had yet to contact.

That, and a distraught Ryan, still upset with me because Bécquer was immortal. As if it was my fault.

But it was I who'd told him, and so he blamed me as he had blamed me for his father's leaving when he was eight. I understood his anger at me was his defense against the pain of finding out Bécquer had lied to him and knew he would eventually work through his pain and forgive me. But not just yet.

I had not asked Ryan if he had seen Bécquer and he had not volunteered any information. My guess was that he had tried and Bécquer had rejected him. I also noticed his showers had gotten longer, an indication that he was dating a new girl. A girl that was not Emily, Madison told me one day out of the blue. "Because I know you don't like Emily and you'll be happy they have broken up."

She was partially right. I liked Emily, but not the fact that she was still doing drugs.

Madison didn't tell me who Ryan's new girl was and I didn't ask. It was an unspoken understanding between us that her first loyalty was to her brother and I knew it would have been useless to challenge that.

*

A week had passed since Bécquer's suicide attempt, when the doorbell rang.

Abby's mother was supposed to pick Madison up and drive both girls to the movies, so I assumed it was Abby at the door. I called to Madison from my study and, when she didn't answer— not surprisingly because I could hear her up in her room, arguing fast and furious on her phone—I got up and opened the door.

It wasn't Abby, but Bécquer who stood outside. Bécquer with a bouquet of roses in one hand and a smile upon his lips.

"Carla," he said and bowed slightly.

"Bécquer?"

"I thought you'd refuse to see me if I called first, so I just came. I hope I'm not interrupting."

I swallowed hard. "No," I mumbled, not sure what his question had been.

"I brought you flowers." His smile had spread over his face now, so his eyes twinkled with mischief.

I looked at the flowers to hide my discomfort at his sudden appearance. They were roses, red roses in a sea of green.

"Roses?"

His smile disappeared. "You don't like roses?"

"Yes, I do."

Bécquer brought the bouquet forward and as I, instinctively, took it from him, a door slammed upstairs and Madison came rushing down calling to me in the hurried voice that announced yet another crisis in her life.

"Mom. Can you drive us? Abby's mom can't take us to the movies—" She stopped as she reached the bottom of the stairs. "Wow! Those are nice! What's the occasion?"

"An excuse to come and see your mother," Bécquer said.

Madison turned to me. "Does that mean you cannot drive me?"

"Actually, I can. Bécquer is leaving."

"Bécquer?" Madison's eyes swept over him with interest. "Ryan's Bécquer?"

"I guess so," Bécquer said, looking amused.

"Ryan's upstairs. Do you want me to get him?"

"No," Bécquer and I said at the same time.

But Madison was already half way upstairs screaming at her brother that Bécquer was waiting for him.

I turned toward Bécquer. "Why have you come?" I asked, risking his stare. "You know it's not safe."

"Please, Carla. Let me talk to you."

"Not now. Not while my children are home."

"Ryan's coming," Madison said joining us again, and, oblivious to my warning stare, invited Bécquer in.

Bécquer shook his head. "Actually, I was leaving."

Madison looked past him to the driveway where his blue BMW was parked. "Is that your car?"

"Yes, it is."

"That is soo cool!"

Bécquer smiled at her. "I can take you and your friend to the movies if you want."

"If your mother agrees," he added as I glowered at him.

"Are you serious? Can I drive?"

"Madison!" I said. "You're fifteen. Of course you cannot drive."

Madison sulked. "I don't know why not. Ryan does."

"Ryan is eighteen and already has his driver's license."

"So what? I know how to drive too and I'm much more mature than him."

"Sorry, Madison. But your mother is right. I'll do the driving." And before I could argue, he took the keys from his pocket and threw them at her. "Wait for me in the car. I'll be there in a minute."

"You can't take Madison," I told him after she dashed out, already punching numbers on her cell "I don't want you to be around my children."

"Because I'm immortal?"

He smiled as I nodded. "Then, there is no problem, because I'm not."

"You are . . . not?"

"No. I'll show you."

Without further invitation, Bécquer came into the house and pulled one rose free from the bouquet I had set upon the table. He winced, set the rose down, and presented his hand to me. A single drop of blood had formed on his thumb.

"You'll see," he said brightly. "I heal slowly, as humans do."

To take this as proof that he was human was ridiculous, but his eagerness had convinced me he was telling the truth. Or was it my own desire blinding me into believing?

"Alexander said your sentence had been revoked," I argued faintly.

Bécquer brought his finger to his lips to stop the blood from spilling, then nodded. "And it has. But I chose to remain human."

"Why?"

The shrill sound of a horn blowing covered his answer.

"I'll tell you later," Bécquer said after the noise stopped. "If you let me come back."

"Are you leaving?"

Ryan's voice startled me. But Bécquer, who had been facing the stairs and must have seen him coming down, only nodded. "I promised to drive your sister to the movies. Unless . . . unless you would drive her for me?"

"Sorry, I don't have time. I have to pick up Rachel in half an hour."

"If you drive your sister, you can borrow my car."

"Really?"

Bécquer nodded. "If your mother would give me a ride home, that is."

Ryan smiled blissfully, and then turned to me. "Thanks, Mom," he said with a quick hug that silenced my complaints.

"You don't mind?" I asked as I watched Ryan disappear inside Bécquer's car.

Bécquer closed the door. "Why? Is he a bad driver?"

"I meant that he's going out with Rachel."

"Why should I? Oh!" He blushed. With a swift movement he grabbed my hands. "What can I do to make you forget my childish behavior of that day? I asked Rachel to be my blood giver only to prove to you that I didn't need you. I never cared for her."

"You used her," I said, releasing my hands from his. "And you hurt her."

"No. I did not. I did not encourage her after that day. I was hurting for you, Carla. I wanted you. I had no desire to seduce her."

"But she cried after you fired her."

"She must have guessed I wanted to kill myself and felt frustrated that she could not help me." He smiled coyly. "Give me some credit, would she have forgotten me already had we been lovers only last week?"

"So irresistible, do you think you are?" I teased him.

"I was, when I was immortal," Bécquer said, serious now. "I am not proud of it. I know my behavior was often selfish and immature. But I've changed since I met you."

"You have?"

"Yes. I brought you flowers."

I frowned. "What is that supposed to prove?"

"It proves I care for you."

"How so?"

"You know how embarrassing it would be for me if you rejected me after I told Ryan that I love you?"

"You told Ryan?"

"Yes. He gave me his permission to ask you out."

"I see," I said. Although in truth, I found the idea of Bécquer asking Ryan's approval beyond ridiculous.

"Ryan loves you," Bécquer said when I didn't elaborate.

"Did he tell you that?"

"No. He mainly complained that you were crazy when he came to see me last Sunday. And by the way, you were not supposed to tell anybody about the immortals, you know? The Elders were not

174

pleased."

"Sorry. Is that why you're still human?"

"No. I told you. That was my choice. I chose to have a human life."

"You had one already."

"Not really. Meeting Lucrezia when I was eleven spoiled it for me. I was her puppet. Or so I used to think. I'm not sure anymore. Maybe I was weak. Maybe things would have been different had I fought her harder. I'm not proud of who I was or what I did during my first human life."

"I think you were brave."

Bécquer frowned.

"I read your journal. I think you were pretty decent as a human. I'm not so sure how I feel about your behavior when you were immortal, though."

"Because of what Beatriz said?"

I shrugged. "And Federico."

Bécquer started. "You discussed my life with Federico?" He seemed dismay.

I nodded.

"Then, there's no hope for me, is there?"

"If I say there is not, would you leave?"

Bécquer stared at me, a deep frown in his forehead. Finally he shook his head. "No. I wouldn't leave. I love you."

"So you said to every one of your many lovers."

"So I may have," Bécquer agreed, then continued eagerly, "I'm sorry, Carla. I can't change the past, but, please, don't reject me just now. I only ask that you give me a chance to show you that I really care."

"What if it doesn't work? What if our relationship ends? Wouldn't you regret then giving up immortality for nothing?"

"It wouldn't have been for nothing. Have you forgotten I wrote my best poems when my love went unrequited. You are my muse, Carla. Thanks to you, my mind is full of stories once again. You have given me a gift more precious than immortality. You will be my muse even if you get tired of me."

"No pressure, then?"

His eyes lit up as a lazy smile curved his lips. "No pressure."

"I suppose, in that case, I could give you a chance. You brought me roses, after all, so it's fair that I let you stay. At least until they wilt."

"And when they wilt, I'll replace them," Bécquer said wrapping his arms around my waist. "And you'll pretend you haven't noticed and let me stay a little longer because, by then, you'll be crazy about me."

"And I'll pretend I've not noticed," I repeated tracing with my fingers the red scar on his neck. "Because I'm crazy about you."

Bécquer took my hand and kissed my fingers one by one.

"Is that human enough for you?" he whispered as another drop of blood welled in his thumb. Without waiting for my answer, he pulled me to him and stole the yes from my lips.

About the Author

I was born in Galicia (northern Spain) and went to college in Madrid, where I finished my Ph.D. in Biology. For the next ten years, I worked as a researcher both in Madrid and at the University of Davis in California.

My writing career started when I came to live in Pennsylvania in the 1990s. Following my first sale, a magazine article on latex allergy, I published four nonfiction books for Chelsea House (Facts on File).

My Young Adult novel, *Two Moon Princess* (the story of a discontented medieval princess, eager to live life on her own terms, who lands in modern day California) was published in 2007 by Tanglewood Press. It was recognized with the bronze award by the *ForeWord Magazine* in the Juvenile fiction category.

Immortal Love is my first adult novel. The Spanish version, *Bécquer eterno*, was included in the Exhibit, Bécquer tan Cerca . . . A través del Arte (Sevilla, May-June 2012).

You can visit me at my blog:
http://carmenferreiroesteban.wordpress.com/
or at my website: *www.carmenferreiroesteban.com.*

For information about my writing/editing/translating services, please go to *www.WriteEditPublish.com.*

In the mood for more Crimson Romance? Check out *The Luminary* by Elle J Rossi at *CrimsonRomance.com*.

Printed in the United States
By Bookmasters